"I'm sorry. I can't wo

She walked briskly to
it open. She had to ge
before he discovered
look at her coal-black hair and eyes that were
changing by the day to look eerily like his and
would instantly know that she was his.

Cold damp air flowed in, making her shiver, but
instead of taking the hint and walking through the
door, Damon paused, and she made the mistake of
looking into his eyes.

Long, tense seconds later, Damon's gaze dropped
to her mouth and the heady tension she had so far
failed to control tightened another notch.

"Damn," he muttered. "I promised myself I wasn't
going to do this."

Zara froze as he cupped her jaw, unwillingly riveted
by the tingling heat that radiated out from that one
point of contact, the unbearably familiar masculine
scents of soap and skin.

* * *

Keeping Secrets is part of
Harlequin Desire's #1 bestselling series,
Billionaires and Babies: Powerful men...wrapped
around their babies' little fingers.

Dear Reader,

Somehow this story got to be all about secrets. A secret baby, a secret identity, a secret past. Throw in an inconvenient attraction for Damon and Zara and things get complicated—and that's *before* baby Rosie arrives.

Rosie is a game changer. Suddenly Damon and Zara are no longer single, but parents, taking on a role that demands new thinking and new priorities. Writing their story, I was reminded of how parenthood challenged me. Suddenly I was in my mother's shoes! Many of the things I had thought were important, and that defined me, dissolved, leaving me with the foundational issues of the heart—love and family and God.

I hope you enjoy Zara and Damon's journey as they unravel the secrets of the past, truly find each other and are smitten by the present reality of gorgeous and vulnerable baby Rosie.

Fiona Brand

FIONA BRAND

KEEPING SECRETS

HARLEQUIN® DESIRE

ISBN-13: 978-1-335-97171-5

Keeping Secrets

Copyright © 2018 by Fiona Gillibrand

Recycling programs for this product may not exist in your area.

For questions and comments about the quality of this book, please contact us at CustomerService@Harlequin.com.

® and TM are trademarks of Harlequin Enterprises Limited or its corporate affiliates. Trademarks indicated with ® are registered in the United States Patent and Trademark Office, the Canadian Intellectual Property Office and in other countries.

Printed in U.S.A.

www.Harlequin.com

Fiona Brand lives in the sunny Bay of Islands, New Zealand. Aside from writing books and gardening, Fiona hosts international students. After a life-changing time in which she met Christ, Fiona has undertaken study for a bachelor of theology, is active in Christ's healing ministry and has become an ordained priest in the Anglican Church.

Books by Fiona Brand

Harlequin Desire

The Pearl House

A Breathless Bride
A Tangled Affair
A Perfect Husband
The Fiancée Charade
Just One More Night
Needed: One Convenient Husband

Billionaires and Babies

Keeping Secrets

Visit her Author Profile page at
Harlequin.com for more titles.

To the Lord, who says, "Come to me, all you who are weary and burdened, and I will give you rest...for I am gentle and humble in heart, and you will find rest for your souls."

–Matthew 11:28–29

Many thanks to Stacy Boyd and Charles Griemsman.

One

The discreet vibration of his cell interrupted Damon Smith's stride as he jogged the hard-packed sand of his private island in New Zealand's Hauraki Gulf.

The conversation was to the point. His younger brother, Ben, was quitting. He would not be in the office tomorrow, or in the foreseeable future.

Reason? He had run off with Damon's pretty blonde personal assistant.

Jaw locked, Damon turned his back on the glare of the setting sun. An icy breeze cooled his overheated skin and flattened his damp T-shirt against the tense muscles of his back, but he barely noticed. For an odd moment sensory perception seemed to fall away and Damon was spun back in time. Almost a year to the day, when another PA, Zara Westlake, had run out on *him*, leaving her job *and his bed*.

Zara. Damon frowned at the image that instantly surfaced. Dark hair, direct blue eyes, finely molded cheekbones made more intriguing by a scattering of freckles. A faintly tip-tilted nose and a firm jaw, all softened by a quirky, generous mouth, which added a fascinating, mercurial depth to a face that was somehow infinitely more riveting than conventional prettiness.

The wind gusted more strongly, the chill registering, as an old wound in his shoulder and another at his hip—both courtesy of his time in the military—stiffened and began to ache. Grimly, Damon dismissed the memories of Zara, annoyed that they still had the power to stop him in his tracks, despite his attempts to put the brief fling in its proper perspective.

After all, their involvement had lasted barely a month. On a scale of one to ten, given that he had once been married for seven years, it shouldn't have registered. Especially since Zara herself, with her usual trademark efficiency, had made it crystal clear she had only ever been interested in a short, very private affair.

"We're in love," Ben helpfully supplied now.

The words *in love* made Damon's jaw tighten. They echoed through a childhood he preferred to forget, one Ben had no knowledge of because he had been lucky enough to be born after the untimely death of their father. Ben had never been around to experience Guy Smith's infidelities or his corrosive temper, the long nights when Damon and his mother had borne the brunt of that temper, and the scars.

"In love." He tried to keep the distaste out of his voice, and failed.

The words dredged up memories of the beautiful women who had hung at the edges of his father's life, expensive women who had demanded diamonds, exotic holidays and credit cards with dizzying limits that had eaten away at the family fortune. Guy Smith had claimed to be "in love" a number of times despite his marriage. When the money had finally run out, his latest mistress had left him. He had ended up in a bar, drunk enough to make the mistake of picking a fight with someone who could hit back. He had been found unconscious on the street the next morning, and had died of a fractured skull on the way to hospital.

When Adeline Smith had gotten the news of her husband's death, she had broken down and cried, but the tears had been ones of relief. Damon, at ten years old, nursing two cracked ribs and a broken jaw courtesy of his attempt to protect his mother from Guy's red-faced fury when he'd discovered they were broke, hadn't shed so much as a tear. Life had been gray and drained of hope. In the instant he heard his father had died, it had felt like stepping out of the shadows into blazing light. Six months later, Ben had been born.

Now, as Ben's only close family, Damon had to tread carefully. His brother hadn't endured the experiences that had shaped Damon. Ben didn't understand how destructive out-of-control emotions could be, and he carelessly fell in and out of love on a regular basis. In a way, Ben's cavalier approach to relationships was an uncomfortable reminder of their father. Although, thankfully, Ben had none of their father's meanness.

Flexing his stiffening shoulder, Damon paced the hard-packed sand of the curving bay, which was punctuated by dark drifts of rock at each end. He forced himself to concentrate on his brother's latest crisis, which this time impacted Damon directly.

For the past eighteen months he had been training Ben to help run their family's sprawling security empire. The one his mother, with the help of her brother, Tyler McCall—Damon's uncle—had pulled from the financial fires of near bankruptcy. Unfortunately, *like their father*, Ben had proven to be spectacularly disinterested in Magnum Security. It was a fact that Damon would have gotten a great deal more done if Ben had not been in the office. His assistant, Emily, however, had been smart, intuitive and almost as efficient as Zara.

With effort, he shook off a further raft of memories and refocused on the problem at hand: saving Ben from himself and retrieving Damon's assistant. Emily was significantly involved in a crucial deal he was working on. At this juncture, it would be nearly impossible to replace her.

"Walk me through this. I didn't think you even liked Emily."

"How would you know? You've had your head buried in the McCall takeover for weeks."

Damon could feel his blood pressure rising. "So has Emily. If you will recall she's my PA."

Although, to put a fine point on it, he had never appointed her to the position. Emily was a temp, the third temp he had employed over the past year while continuing to interview numerous candidates, both male and female, some with impressive degrees. Unfortunately, not one of them had possessed the exacting qualities required for the position. Qualities that had been oddly defined in Zara and which he had not realized he needed until she left him.

"Uh, not any longer. Check your email and you'll find Emily's resignation."

A boarding call echoed through the phone, informing Damon that Ben and Emily were already at the airport.

Damon kept a lid on his frustration. He could live with the inconvenience of losing Emily. What really worried him was what was happening to Ben. The partying and dating aside, he was becoming immersed in the darker, undisciplined passions that had overtaken their father. Passions that had even extended to Tyler McCall, who had become the CEO of Magnum Security and the boys' guardian following Adeline's death from cancer when Damon was fourteen and Ben just four. As stable as Tyler, an ex-SEAL and intelligence expert had seemed, in his late forties he had fallen for a spectacularly beautiful model, then died along with her in a car accident on the romantic Mediterranean island of Medinos.

Damon's chest tightened at the memory of the loss that, four years ago, had hit him hard. Tyler had been the father Guy Smith should have been. He had been a safe haven for both Damon and Ben until he had been ensnared by Petra Hunt, an aging model turned A-list party girl.

To lose Tyler, whose watchwords had been *reliability* and *common sense*, to the kind of liaison that had gone hand in glove with Damon's father's degenerate lifestyle… It had, to put it mildly, shaken Damon.

Damned if he'd let Ben fall into the same trap.

Damon's fingers tightened on the phone. Technically, Ben had not run off with Emily yet; they were both still at the airport. There was a chance to nip the relationship in the bud if Damon kept his cool. "Don't board the flight. I can be at the airport in an hour—we can talk this through."

"There's nothing to talk about," Ben said curtly. "Emily and I have been seeing each other for the past month. Long enough to decide that this is something special."

"You're only twenty—"

"Old enough to make my own decisions. Last I heard, I could go to war at eighteen if I wanted. You were younger when you married Lily."

Damon's brows jerked together at the mention of his ex-wife. "The two situations don't equate."

"Why? Because Lily left you?"

For a vibrating moment Damon was confronted by a past he took great pains to avoid thinking about, because it highlighted the singular difficulty he had with relationships. There hadn't been one thing wrong with Lily. She had been beautiful, intelligent and sweet-natured and he had *liked* her, all good reasons to choose her as his wife. Unfortunately, he had never been able to give Lily the two things she had decided she wanted from him *after* the wedding. First, that he would fall in love with her. Second, that he would give her the children she had decided were now a deal breaker.

There was a loaded pause. "Or is it because you slept with your assistant last year," Ben asked softly, "and you've suddenly decided *that's* a forbidden sin?"

Damon stopped dead in his tracks. Flashes of the stark, heated passion Zara had unlocked in him, and which he had constantly failed to control, rushed back at him, making his chest tighten. "How could you know about that?"

Zara had insisted they keep the liaison secret. She had made it clear she couldn't work for him if people knew they were involved. Damon had complied even though he hadn't liked the condition. It had smacked of his father's illicit affairs. Emotion might be a no-go area, but Damon preferred to keep his sexual relationships straightforward and aboveboard.

Ben's tone was impatient. "Zara is Emily's agent. Emily put two and two together."

Damon's stomach tensed as more memories of Zara surfaced. In every way, Zara was his ex-wife's polar opposite. Exactly the kind of woman he usually took care to avoid, because of the subtle, locked-down sensuality that was just a little too interesting. Zara had been dark and curvaceous, where Lily had been blonde, athletic and slender. The differences hadn't stopped at physical appearance. From the first moment, Zara had been a vivid, fascinating mixture of efficiency, quirky humor and unexpected passion.

Their connection had blindsided them both.

"The two situations are not the same."

"Right on to that. What Emily and I share is more than just convenient sex."

An image of Zara lying in bed, dark satiny hair spread over the pillow, blue eyes veiled with mysteries and secrets, assaulted him. Convenient sex? There had been nothing convenient about it. The words that sprang to mind were more along the lines of *hot, reckless*.

Addictive.

The same brand of intense, unruly passion that had ruined his father and Tyler and which had kept Damon awake nights because he had vowed it would never control him.

A clarifying thought that made sense of Ben and Emily's elopement suddenly occurred to Damon. He could kick himself for not thinking of it before. "Emily's pregnant."

Ben made a sound of disbelief. "Emily's not the one who got pregnant."

Not the one who got pregnant.

The words seemed to hang in the air. Suddenly, like a piece of a puzzle falling neatly into place, Zara's abrupt exit from Damon's life, her disappearance for months, made perfect sense.

She had left because she had been pregnant. With *his* child.

Damon sucked in a deep breath and tried to think, tried to orient himself. He felt like he'd been kicked in the chest.

If Zara had had a baby—and by now, over a year on, the baby would be four months old—why hadn't she told him?

Admittedly, they hadn't known each other long, six weeks in total.

Long enough to get messily involved and for Damon to break a whole list of personal rules.

Long enough that he'd had trouble forgetting her. That he'd broken his last intact rule, a rule that should have been inviolable. Instead of letting Zara go and regaining his equilibrium, *his distance*, when she left town, he had gone after her.

He had tracked her to a small cottage in the South Island city of Dunedin. On the verge of knocking on her front door, he had abruptly come to his senses. He had known that if he walked through that door they would be in bed within minutes. Added to that, if he

continued an affair that had become dangerously irresistible, he risked becoming engaged to and marrying a
woman who was the exact opposite of the kind of wife
he needed. A passionate, addictive, unpredictable lover
who had made it clear she had no interest in a committed relationship.

Disgusted with the obsession that had clearly gotten an unhealthy grip on him, he had walked away. The
only problem was, he had not been able to stay away.
Months later, when he had discovered Zara had opened
her own employment agency in town, instead of steer-
ing clear, he had requested that his office manager ditch
the large, established firm that usually fulfilled their
employment needs and start using Zara's agency.

His fingers tightened on the cell. "How long have
you known that Zara had a baby?"

Ben made an exasperated sound. "Right at this moment I'm not sure if you're burying your head in the
sand out on that fortress island of yours or if you really didn't know. If Emily was expecting my child, *I*
wouldn't be afraid of fatherhood."

Fatherhood.

Damon stared bleakly at the misty line where sky
met sea. Unwittingly, Ben had gone straight for the
jugular, exposing a truth Damon had no wish to con-
front. The whole issue of fatherhood was something
he usually avoided, because it entailed facing a past he
had gone to a great deal of trouble to bury and forget.

It meant coming to grips with another relationship for which he was not ready or equipped.

Lily's words when she had stormed out of their apartment came back to haunt him. *I must have been out of my mind thinking I could live with a man who approaches marriage as if it's some kind of business contract and who doesn't want kids, ever!*

He took another deep breath but, even so, when he spoke his voice was raspy. "The baby's...all right?"

Ben said something short and flat. "You really didn't know. Well, that takes the cake. You're a security guru. You wrote the book on surveillance techniques and you produce software for half a dozen governments, and you don't know when your ex-girlfriend has your child? I thought you didn't want to know, because you don't want kids. Lily said enough about the sub—"

"Don't bring Lily into this." The response was automatic, because every thought was blasted away by the fact that Zara had given birth to his child.

The one outcome he had taken care to avoid, *except on one notable occasion*, had happened.

He was a father.

A final boarding call echoed down the phone.

"I've gotta go," Ben muttered. "Look, I'm sorry about breaking the news about Zara and the baby like this. The fact was, I thought you did know but were... you know, *avoiding* the whole issue." There was a rustling sound as if Ben was holding the phone awkwardly jammed to his ear as he surrendered his boarding pass.

"Emily was fairly sure you didn't know. She seemed to think it was more that you lack emotional intelligence… whatever that means."

There was a feminine yelp in the background along with a further rustling noise as if Ben had jammed the phone against his chest to muffle the sound for a few seconds.

Ben's voice came back, loud and clear. "Anyway, I think we both know that trying to turn me into an executive wasn't working. I told you right from the start that the kind of locked-down life you lead isn't for me. I want to travel and do something with my fine arts degree. Anything but add up soulless numbers all day and stare at computer code, which, by the way, I will never understand. Don't try to find us. I'll send a postcard…eventually."

A click signaled the call had been terminated.

Damon slipped the phone back into the pocket of his sweatpants. There was no point in running after Ben now. The boarding calls meant that whatever flight Ben and Emily had booked, they would be airborne before he could pull the strings needed to either detain them or delay the flight. That was no doubt the reason Ben had rung just before the flight left. Damon guessed he was lucky that Ben, who had been kicking against Damon's authority for the past year, had called at all.

Feeling like an automaton, Damon went back over the conversation. Ben's crack about his lack of emotional intelligence grated. Apparently, he had missed two major cues in his life, Ben's utter lack of interest in Magnum Security and the fact that Damon had fathered a child, *despite Zara assuring him there was no chance of a pregnancy.*

He tried to remember the exact words Zara had used immediately after they'd had crazy, passionate, unprotected sex. She had dragged on a robe and escaped to the bathroom, pausing to send him an irritatingly neutral smile, before assuring him that he had no need to worry.

He had taken that to mean Zara had taken care of contraception. But now he knew it could also have meant that his assistant, in her usual brisk, efficient way, had been stating her intention to take full responsibility if there was a pregnancy.

Cold water splashed his ankles and Damon became aware that the tide had advanced and water was now surging around his shoes. Still absorbed with his thoughts, he strolled up the beach and headed for his house. Perched on a headland, the large multilevel house seemed to grow from the dark cliffs, stark and spare and a little forbidding. Built of stone, it reminded him of the medieval fortress Tyler had owned on the Mediterranean island of Medinos and which Damon had spent his adolescence exploring.

Fatherhood. The realization sank in a little deeper.

Damon turned to stare across the water in the direction of Auckland's cityscape, the first glimmer of evening lights visible in the distance. Somewhere across the water existed a child who, in a profound, unassailable way, belonged to him.

Just beyond the breaking waves a sleek gannet arrowed into the water, then surfaced with a silvery fish in its beak. Damon drew in a lungful of cold air as he struggled with imperatives that were as opposite as black and white. He had long ago decided that fatherhood was not for him, but fate had intervened and he was caught and held as fast as the small, flapping fish. He could not turn his back on his child.

The sun was sinking fast, the last burnished glow infusing the clear winter air with rose and gold. The sea breeze had dropped, leaving the water glassily smooth.

He did not understand why Zara had chosen to cut him out of his child's life, but that would soon change. In the methodical way of his mind, Damon began to formulate a plan to meet with Zara and discover what he could about the child. Although the practical to-do list seemed cold and antiseptic when he considered exactly what it meant—confronting his ex-lover about the child they had made together. And he knew exactly when that had happened—the first time they had made love.

As Damon climbed the steep cliff path to his house, memories flickered, vivid and irresistible.

Torrential rain pounding down as he held his jacket over Zara's head to shelter her as he dropped her home after a late business dinner. He shook out the wet jacket in the dimness of her porch. She laughed as she swept soaked hair back from her forehead. With her dark hair gleaming with moisture, her cheeks flushed, suddenly she was quite startlingly beautiful.

There was a moment when he bent his head, a split second before their mouths touched, when she could have stepped away and didn't. Instead, her breath hitched, her fingers closed on the lapels of his jacket and she lifted up on her toes for his kiss.

He caught the scent of her skin and desire closed around him like heated manacles. Sensation shuddered through him in waves as they kissed for long, spellbinding minutes. They made it to her bedroom, just.

He used a condom the first and even the second time, but in the hour before dawn, waking to Zara making slow, exquisite love to him, and caught in that strange halfway state between dream and reality, he did not.

The unprotected lovemaking had happened with blinding speed, over almost before he realized it, but that did not negate his responsibility. Zara's pregnancy had been his fault.

Damon climbed the steps to his house and paused in the shelter of the heavy stone portico, which protected the entryway from the wind. Peeling out of his wet shoes, he pushed open the heavy, ancient door made of thick oak and bands of iron that he had imported from Medinos and headed for his shower. After drying off, he pulled on soft, faded jeans with the fluid economy of movement he had learned during his years with the military in Afghanistan and the Middle East.

Not bothering with a shirt, Damon padded into his

cavernous bedroom, found his laptop and keyed in the GPS program his firm used as a security measure for the company's top executives. He typed in his brother's phone number. Instantly a map materialized along with a tracking icon, which indicated that Ben was over the Pacific Ocean, just northeast of Auckland. It was somehow typical that Ben, with his utter disinterest in all things to do with Magnum Security, had been careless enough to forget that his phone could be tracked.

Damon checked the time then rang Walter, his head of security and one of his most trusted employees. Minutes later, Ben's flight details were confirmed. He was headed for the island of Medinos, and would, no doubt, be staying in the clifftop fortress Tyler had left to him and Ben jointly.

Retrieving his cell, he found the only number for Zara that he had, her employment agency. After a moment of hesitation, he dialed. In the past two months, ever since he had discovered that Zara had opened her own agency, apart from picking up his initial call, he had invariably found himself shunted through to her answering service. His jaw compressed when, as usual, the call went straight through to voice mail. He left a terse message and set the phone down on his bedside table.

Stepping out onto his balcony, he studied the gray clouds building overhead, blotting out the first scattering of stars. Ben had been right in pointing out the irony that Damon specialized in designing hardware and software to collect, unlock and decode information, and yet he could not unlock the mystery of the woman who had shared his bed and then attempted to disappear with all the skill of a master spy.

Cold droplets spattered Damon's broad shoulders as he turned from the darkening view, strolled through to the kitchen and lifted the lid on the casserole Walter's wife, Margot, had left for him. Not for the first time, he was keenly aware of the utter emptiness of his house.

For years he had been living in a kind of deep freeze. Just over a year ago, when Zara had strolled into his office in a beige jacket and skirt that on most women would have looked shapeless and boring, but on her had somehow looked sexy, the thaw had been instant and profound.

He had wanted her. If he was ruthlessly honest, that was also the reason he had reconnected with Zara again when he found out she had opened her own employment agency. To date, he had resisted what he'd come to view as a fatal attraction, but that was about to change. The knowledge that Zara had had his child had kicked away some invisible barrier. They were linked in the most primal, intimate way a man and woman could be linked and he was no longer prepared to tolerate the distance she seemed to prefer.

From now on, they were playing by his rules.

He had not forgotten Ben. As Ben's only close relative and the trustee of Ben's inheritance, Damon's course of action was clear. He needed to retrieve his brother before Ben did something completely irresponsible, like get married to a woman he had only known for a few weeks.

The retrieval of Ben, as luck would have it, dovetailed with Damon's need to gain access to his child. Zara Westlake stood at the center of both issues, which meant that, whether she liked it or not, she would have to meet with him face-to-face.

Out of the murk of the first two objectives, a third emerged. Despite Zara's betrayal, despite the grip the past still had on his life, he needed one more thing.

Zara Westlake back in his bed.

Two

A soft chime, indicating that a much-needed client had just opened the door of Zara's fledgling employment agency, diverted her attention from her four-month-old baby, Rosie. Thankfully, after a marathon effort to get Rosie to nap, her tiny daughter had finally drifted into a restless slumber.

Anxious to snag her client before he or she lost interest and decided to take their very valuable business elsewhere, Zara tiptoed out of the smallest interview room, which today doubled as Rosie's makeshift nursery. Makeshift, because normally, when Zara was working, Rosie was in day care. But, because Rosie had been a little off-color, the center hadn't wanted to take her, so Zara had planned to work from home while she kept an eye on her daughter. However, that arrangement had crashed and burned when her assistant, Molly, had called in sick at the last minute, meaning that Zara had been forced to bring Rosie to the office.

It wasn't until she had gently closed the door behind her that Zara realized she had left her high heels, which she had slipped out of while she had fed and changed Rosie, behind her desk. Added to that, her hair, once smoothed into an immaculate French pleat, was now disheveled from the playful grip of Rosie's fingers.

Pinning a smoothly professional smile on her face, she turned to her client. In that instant, the room seemed to whirl, reminding her of the last month of pregnancy when bouts of dizziness would hit out of the blue.

Disbelief froze her in place as Zara's gaze traveled from the rock-solid shape of a masculine jaw, with the hint of a five o'clock shadow, to the scar that sliced across one cheekbone, a fascinating counterpart to the damaged line of a once-aquiline nose. Her own jaw taut, she braced herself for the impact of the magnetic silvery gaze, which had always put her in mind of that of a very large, very focused wolf.

Her heart slammed against the wall of her chest. A complicated mix of panic, edged with another purely feminine reaction she refused to acknowledge.

He had found her.

Damon Smith.

Six foot two inches of scarred, muscular, reclusive billionaire standing in her tiny office, taking all the air, his sleek shoulders broad enough that they stretched the dark fabric of a very expensive black coat.

A stomach-churning anxiety kicked in as she wondered why he was here. Damon Smith had the kind of wealth and power that meant he did not have to leave his private island or his penthouse office unless he chose to do so. There was a small army of devoted, ex-military employees who had been with him for years and who were ready and willing to do his slightest bidding.

Damon turning up in her office was significant.

Cold air gusted, shaking the windows. Predictably, her door, which had a malfunctioning catch, flung open. Damon caught the door before it could bang against the wall, his dark coat swirling like a mantle as he did so, cloaking its owner in the shadows and secrets that permeated his life. Public secrets due to his work. Private secrets, which she was privy to and wished she wasn't, because they also scored *her* life.

He closed the door and tested it to make sure the catch had engaged. His gaze, now distinctly irritable, pinned her again. "You need to get that fixed."

"It's on my list."

Along with fixing the leaky tap in the tiny bathroom and replacing some of the light fittings, which looked like they had been salvaged from a Second World War junk sale. Knowing her landlord, they probably had.

Keeping a neutral smile fixed firmly in place, Zara girded herself to hold Damon's gaze with the equanimity she had learned in an elite finishing school in Switzerland, all paid for by her gorgeous, restless, jet-setting supermodel mother, Petra Atrides, who had been known in the fashion and media worlds as Petra Hunt. A practiced composure, which had been put to the test by the paparazzi when Petra had plunged to her death along with her new fiancé—Damon's uncle Tyler McCall.

Not that Damon knew any of that, which was the way she wanted to keep it. There was no way Damon would believe she had not known who he was when she accepted the job as his personal assistant and then practically flung herself into his bed. Not when he discovered she was Petra Hunt's daughter *and* had given birth to his child.

The wind buffeted the front door again, the force of it actually making the lights flicker, but this time the door held.

Damon took in her small office in one sweeping glance. "So this is where you've been hiding out."

"What do you mean, 'hiding out'?"

Although the fact that she *had* been in hiding for the past thirteen months, hiding a pregnancy and now a baby, put an annoying blush on her cheeks.

Damon's expression was deceptively mild. "You haven't been answering your phone or returning calls, and the address you gave me over the phone a couple of months ago is incorrect. I've spent the past half hour walking the streets and questioning shop owners who had never heard of you. It wasn't until I went online and checked your social media site that I managed to get your real address."

Zara struggled to control another surge of heat to her cheeks. Weeks ago, when Damon had contacted her out of the blue, she hadn't meant to give him incorrect information. In a moment of panic, thinking that he had somehow found out about Rosie, the transposed figures had just tumbled out of her. But neither should he, a CEO, have been even remotely interested in the whereabouts of her office. When she had agreed to take on Magnum Security as a client, she had only done so because she had desperately needed the money and on the condition that all of her dealings were with Damon's dry-as-dust business manager, Howard Prosser. In theory she should never have had to deal with Damon, period.

She stiffened at the image of the extraordinarily wealthy and private Damon Smith walking the streets and questioning shop owners.

Hunting her.

A sharp little thrill shot down her spine. Instantly, her jaw firmed. That was the kind of feminine reaction toward Damon that she had never been able to afford, because he was, literally, the one man she should not want and could not have in her life.

Aside from being a link to a past she was determined to leave behind, she had found out that Damon was also the trustee of his uncle's estate. He had requested, through his lawyers, that she, as Angel Atrides—her name before she had legally changed it to Zara Westlake—sign a legal document relinquishing any claim on Tyler's estate in exchange for a one-off, extremely offensive cash offer.

Raw with grief, insulted and *hurt*, Zara had refused the offer and had refused to sign the horrible legal agreement. She had been sickened by the tactics of a family who had obviously bought into the media hype around her mother as a model who was past her prime and who had inveigled her way into Tyler's über-rich, normally sensible life. No doubt Damon believed that Angel Atrides was just as trashy and opportunistic, and that a chunk of cash and a legal agreement was a necessary insurance against her ever darkening his doorstep or, horror of horrors, trying to make a claim on Tyler's fortune.

Once again, the calculated risk of accepting Magnum as a client made her heart pound. Her chest seized on a sudden thought. Could Damon know about Rosie?

Last night he had left a message on her answering service, a terse command to call him back. It was something she had deliberately left for Molly to attend to.

Summoning a smooth smile, and trying to control her racing pulse, Zara made it to the safe haven of her desk. "I'm sorry you had trouble finding me."

Feeling pinned by his gaze, she opened a drawer on the pretext that she wanted to check the address on her business cards. Although, she knew there was nothing wrong with her cards. Her mother might have been a creative, artistic personality who resisted being organized and hated dealing with numbers, but Zara was her polar opposite. A perfectionist and a details person, she preferred to lead, not follow, and she liked to get things right.

The flush on her cheeks seemed to grow more heated as she jerkily closed the drawer on her stack of perfectly aligned, perfectly correct business cards. "I'm sorry you somehow ended up with the wrong address."

Grim amusement flickered at the corners of Damon's mouth. "The number was reversed. But something tells me you already knew that."

Her chin jerked up. "What are you insinuating?"

Damon shrugged. "Thirteen months ago, you quit your job and disappeared. For the past couple of months, ever since I discovered you had opened up your own employment agency, apart from picking up my first call, you've consistently failed to return my calls—"

"You know I prefer to work via email. Besides, all the correspondence and contracts go through Howard."

He glanced around her office again, his gaze briefly settling on the door of the interview room where Rosie was sleeping. "Maybe the address you gave me was a genuine mistake."

But his tone told her he didn't believe that.

His gaze shifted thoughtfully back to the door of the interview room and a sharp jolt of adrenaline made her heart pound.

She was suddenly certain that he *knew*.

A little feverishly, she straightened piles of paper

that did not need straightening. The only way Damon could have found out about Rosie was through Emily, although her contact with Emily had been minimal, two interviews and a couple of phone updates. She was not even sure Emily was aware that Zara had a baby. Of course, there were other ways he could have pried into her life. Given that he was in the security and surveillance business and had once been some kind of Special Forces agent in the military, she was certain he could find out whatever he wanted.

Damon's gaze skimmed her neatly arranged office and Zara did her best to conceal her relief that he was no longer concentrated on the door to the interview room in which Rosie was sleeping. When it came to Damon, usually, she erred on the side of fighting, but today running was at the top of the list—with Rosie tucked invisibly under one arm so he would not uncover that particular guilty secret.

Shockingly, his gaze touched on hers before shifting and she realized he had noticed her hair. She took a calming breath and willed her heart rate to slow. There was nothing wrong with messy hair. It was a windy day. Her hair could have gotten disheveled when she'd gone out for coffee.

A weird part of her acknowledged that she had always known this could happen, that one day her most lucrative client, who also happened to be the father of her child, would walk into her office and she would have to deal with him face-to-face. But, not now, not today, when she was struggling from lack of sleep and with Rosie just feet away in the next room.

The last thing either of them needed was to be inescapably linked by Rosie. A small shudder went through Zara at the thought of the media attention that would erupt once it was found out that Petra Hunt's daughter, using a new identity, had had a child with Tyler McCall's nephew. They would come after her; they would come after Rosie. And Damon, apart from making it crystal clear that Zara was not welcome in his life, would hate that she had fooled him.

On cue, a small, snuffling sound came from the interview room. Zara's heart sped up. Lately, Rosie, who was usually a very good sleeper, was waking up after just a few minutes of restless slumber. A little desperately, she reached for a random file and slapped it down on the desk, trying to make enough noise that Damon would not hear Rosie. "So, now that you've found me, what can I do for you? Is there a problem with one of the employees I sent to you? Troy? Or Harold?"

Troy was young, just eighteen, with tattoos and a brow piercing, but he was bright and earnest. Zara had thought he would be perfect for Damon's IT team. Harold had been an older public servant who had failed to find a job through other employment agencies, owing to a rather unfortunate skin condition, and in desperation had come to Zara. She had found a place for him in Damon's accounts department.

Damon frowned slightly, as if he didn't know who

either Troy or Harold were, then his face cleared. "They're fine, as far as I know. *This* is the problem."

He dropped the tabloid newspaper, which he had been carrying under one arm, on her desk. It was folded open at a tacky gossip columnist's page.

She drew a calming breath and forced herself to study a grainy black-and-white photo of Damon's younger brother, Ben, who had his arm flung around Emily's slim waist. The blaring caption, Magnum Security Heir's Hot Affair with Blonde Temp, practically leaped off the page.

Snatching up the paper, she skimmed the story—which was the stuff of her nightmares—with growing horror. Thankfully, the detail was minimal. To her relief, the name of her employment agency had not been mentioned...yet.

She took a closer look at the photograph. Details she had not noticed first off finally registered. Emily's hair seemed longer and curlier. Gone were the subtle makeup and low-key suits, the crisp blouses that had seemed to summarize Zara's star temp as sensible, trustworthy and professional. Emily looked younger and a touch bohemian. She certainly no longer looked like the poster girl for Westlake Employment Agency.

Zara quickly read the sketchy article. Of course, the journalist had painted Emily as a fortune-hunting employee and Ben as the kind of high-powered playboy businessman who was only interested in a quick fling and who would not be easily caught by a mere office girl.

Compassion for Emily mixed with a surge of outrage and a fierce desire to protect her protégé. Just because Emily had fallen for Ben and decided to make the best of herself did not make her a cheap, trashy opportunist. Zara had lost count of the times the papers had portrayed her mother as cheap and on the make, when the truth was that her mother had been so gorgeous she had literally had to fend off men. And yes, some of those men had been breathtakingly rich.

When Petra died, the behavior of the tabloids and women's magazines had worsened. They had smeared her reputation even more before turning their malicious spotlight on Zara. Although, luckily, Petra had always made sure Zara was hidden from the media, so their store of background information had been meager. Most of the photos they'd had were blurred shots of Zara as a child or as a plump teenager taken through telephoto lenses.

Horrified and frightened by the relentless pursuit of the media, Zara had ditched her degree and disappeared. Angel Atrides, the fictional spoiled party girl the media seemed intent on creating, had become the ordinary, invisible person she longed to be—Zara Westlake. Zara had been her paternal grandmother's name, Westlake her maternal grandmother's maiden name.

Her mother's cousin Phoebe Westlake, a sharp-edged accountant who was ill with leukemia, had provided the hideout Zara needed in the South Island city of Dunedin while she had painstakingly reinvented her life. Which had made it all the more frustrating when, almost three years later, with a new name and a degree in business management—in effect a new life—Phoebe's last act before she had died had been to secure Zara a job interview with the nephew of Tyler McCall.

Not that Zara had made *that* connection until after she had taken the job, because Damon's surname, Smith, was so neutral and ordinary that she hadn't suspected the link. To further muddy the waters, Damon was reclusive by nature, avoiding the media. It hadn't been until two weeks into her job and *after* she had made the mistake of sleeping with Damon, that he had handed her a takeover bid for Tyler McCall's electric company.

She had finally understood exactly who Damon was.

As much as she needed to sit down now, Zara remained standing. Once again, the desire to run was uppermost, but she instantly dismissed that option. In setting up her business after Rosie was born she had made a stand. She was over running.

She was tired of giving up things that were important, like home and friendships and career choices, and having to start fresh somewhere else. Having to *be* someone else. If she ran now, she would have to give up her cozy rented cottage, which was just a twenty-minute commute from her office. She would have to abandon her business, which she loved with passion, because, finally, all of her study and hard work had paid off and she had something of substance that was *hers*. Plus, if she walked away now she would be deeply in debt, with no way to repay it.

The thought of defaulting on her business loan made her stomach tighten. It was a sharp reminder of exactly why she had buckled and taken on Damon as a client in the first place. It had been a huge risk, but if she hadn't, she would have gone under. Damon, against all odds, was her most lucrative client and had taken on a staggering number of personnel, most of them temps, which meant she continued to accrue fees.

Her jaw firmed. Right now, she could not cope with another debt. It had taken her years to pay off her mother's funeral expenses. However, not running meant she might have to face the press, and probably sooner rather than later.

The way she saw it, her only viable option was damage control. Luckily, due to her current line of work, she had become quite skilled at it. Refolding the paper so she no longer had to look at the damaging article or the gleeful smile of the gossip columnist, and utterly relieved that the situation with Ben and Emily was Damon's reason for seeking her out, she directed a brisk glance at him. "When did they leave?"

"Last night, on a scheduled flight. Which is why the tabloids got hold of the story."

If it had been the firm's private jet, the press wouldn't have gotten a look in, but Damon would have been notified. Damon had been caught by surprise, which meant

Ben had kept his plans secret. That being the case, it was entirely possible, given that Zara hadn't known about the relationship, that Damon had not, either.

Light glimmered at the end of a very long, very dark tunnel. Damon had clearly bought into the tabloid story, but there were other constructions that could apply to Ben and Emily leaving the country together—constructions that did not place the blame on either Emily or Westlake Employment.

Mind working quickly, Zara examined and discarded a number of options, finally settling on attack as the best form of defense. "It's highly irregular that Ben has taken Emily out of the country." She lifted her chin, but even so, in her bare feet, her gaze was only just level with Damon's throat. She tried not to be fascinated by a very interesting pulse along the side of his jaw. "When might I expect my temp to be returned?"

Damon's brows jerked together. "Emily was not kidnapped."

Surreptitiously, Zara felt around with her toes for her shoes. "I didn't say *kidnapped*, exactly."

Damon crossed his arms over his chest, which only served to make him seem even larger and more ticked off. "You're implying that she has been coerced in some way. Since Emily, at twenty-six, is older than Ben by a good six years, I doubt any coercion was involved."

The age twenty-six hit an unexpected nerve. It was the same age she had been when she'd had the wild, silly affair with Damon. Heat surged into her cheeks.

It was hard to believe it had been little more than a year ago. So much had happened it felt like centuries had passed. "You're right, at twenty-six, she should have known better."

Zara only wished she had.

Damon's gaze clashed with hers. Zara dragged her gaze free, but not before her fiery irritation was replaced by other, more disturbing sensations coiling low in the pit of her stomach.

Upset and annoyed at the intense, too-familiar awareness that had hit her out of left field, as if they were still connected—*still lovers*—in desperation, Zara recommenced the search for her shoes. She finally located them in the shadowed recesses beneath her desk. Relieved to have a distraction, she bent down and snatched them up. Unlike her suit, which was black and neatly tailored, the shoes were a tad subversive, a gorgeous sea blue that unashamedly matched her eyes.

On the subject of eyes, she thought grimly, *note to self, never look into Damon's eyes for too long*. Apparently, despite dismissing him from her life and putting a great deal of effort into forgetting about him completely, even one second was too long.

With an effort of will, Zara smoothed out her expression, but there was another tiny issue that was bugging her. "And Emily being older than Ben by several years would, of course, make her the predatory one." She could not forget that the paparazzi had nicknamed Petra, who had been several years older than Tyler, "the

Huntress." As if Petra had been cold and calculating, and had deliberately set out to ensnare a rich lover, when Zara knew that it had been Tyler who had pursued Petra.

Damon frowned. "I wasn't trying to imply that Emily was predatory because she's older—"

"Good, because we both know Ben is something of a party animal."

Damon seemed briefly riveted by the shoes, and she realized she was brandishing them in front of her like a weapon. Taking a deep breath, she placed the shoes on the floor and methodically slipped them on. The heels gave her an extra inch and half, which wasn't nearly enough.

Damon's gaze clashed with hers again, the hard edge tempered by something she had never seen before, something new, an intent curiosity, as if he was logging the changes in her and taking stock in a completely masculine way.

She suppressed her automatic panic that Damon would somehow equate her extra curves with motherhood. She had to keep reminding herself that Damon's focus was on rescuing Ben from Emily; he didn't know Zara had had his child. In any case, the obvious explanation for her more rounded shape was a whole lot simpler, that she had just put on a little weight.

Damon's expression shuttered. "You know very well that I meant Ben couldn't take a woman like Emily anywhere she didn't want to go."

In the midst of what was for Zara a stressful encounter,

Damon's flat statement informed her that he knew exactly what she was trying to achieve with her line of reasoning. It was also a reminder of just why she had fallen for him in the first place. Most people, quite rightly, viewed him as cold and formidable, even dangerous. But that had not been Zara's experience. As an employer she had found him to be demanding but utterly straightforward. Far from being intimidated, she had found that, on a purely feminine level, she had liked his air of command and the knowledge that, in a company full of alpha males, Damon was the scariest, most alpha of them all.

Grudgingly, she conceded Damon's point that Emily was not the type to be coerced. "Even so, this is out of character for her. If she had wanted to take time off, she would have emailed me or left a message."

Although the instant Zara said the words she remembered that she had seen an email from Emily but hadn't opened it because she'd been so busy with Rosie and walk-in clients.

Damon extracted his cell from his pocket, flicked the screen with his thumb, then placed the phone down on her desk so she could see Emily's email. "Her resignation is there in black and white."

Shocked, Zara flipped her laptop open and scrolled down her inbox to confirm that she had received almost exactly the same message. Hers, however, was peppered with apologies and assurances that Emily would ring once they got to Medinos.

Medinos. Zara tensed even further.

The island was exotic and beautiful and was popularly styled as the Mediterranean isle of romance. It had also been Zara's home as a child while her father, Angelo Atrides, the last *conte* of the once-aristocratic but now-impoverished Atrides line, had been alive. But in Zara's experience, since Angelo's death when she was barely seven years old, the only thing that had come out of Medinos was trouble. "I don't know why Emily would run off with Ben. They're total opposites."

Ben, though ridiculously handsome, was too young for Emily and a little spoiled. He hadn't been born with a silver spoon in his mouth; it had been platinum.

While Zara had been reading, Damon had been pacing around her office, examining her walls with their job-notice boards and career displays, reminding her of nothing so much as a large wolf on the prowl. "It would seem Emily's decided to take a break from work with Ben—"

"You think this is just a holiday?" Damon's tone was laced with disbelief.

Still upset at the physicality of her reaction to Damon, a reaction that should have been as dead as a doornail by now, Zara snatched up the newspaper and stared at the grainy photo. "What else could you call it? I don't see an engagement ring, so they're not eloping—"

Damon's gaze pinned her. "Damn right. Ben will not be marrying Emily."

The flat denial, which somehow implied that Emily was not good enough to marry Ben, flicked Zara on the raw. "Ben should be so lucky. Emily is smart and mature. Apart from this…*error* of judgment, she's an exemplary personal assistant."

"If there's been an error of judgment, then that also applies to Ben."

Zara slapped the newspaper back down on the desk. "Why does it always come back to that? You know, people can simply fall in love. When my father died, it took my mother years to find—" She stopped, appalled by what she had almost given away.

There was a moment of vibrating silence. "What do you mean by 'Why does it always come back to that?'"

Relieved that Damon had bypassed her comment about her mother, Zara blurted out her thoughts. "Isn't that what rich men automatically think? That women are attracted by their wealth?"

She cringed the moment the words were out, because she didn't actually believe that about all wealthy men.

Damon's gaze pinned her. "Is that what you believed about me?"

Three

The soft, flat question made her chest go tight and her heart pound. Damon zeroing in on their short, secretive fling was disorienting when a moment ago they had been firmly focused on Ben and Emily.

Zara found herself once more staring at the pulse throbbing along the side of Damon's jaw as she desperately tried to find a neutral way out of a conversation that had careered out of control.

She took a deep breath and decided on the truth. After all, what did it matter now? "Yes."

A curious satisfaction registered in Damon's gaze. "So that's why you didn't want a relationship. You thought I would think you were after my money."

It was only part of the truth.

The whole of it was that if Damon ever found out her real identity, he wouldn't just think she was after his money, he would be certain of it. Although, the irony was that, from the first moment she had met him, she couldn't have cared less about his wealth.

When she had walked into the interview with Damon, his remote gaze had connected with hers and for a split second she'd had a weird premonition that everything was about to change. She could not explain exactly what the phenomenon was, just that for her, at least, it had been instant, visceral and electric. Like a piece of flotsam caught in a powerful current, she had allowed herself to be swept along and had accepted the job. Two weeks later, she had ended up in Damon's bed.

Determined to redirect the conversation back to the situation with Emily and Ben, and hustle Damon out of the door before Rosie woke up, Zara briskly stepped around her desk and busied herself tidying piles of pamphlets that did not need tidying. "I'm sorry for the inconvenience of Emily taking an unplanned leave of absence—"

"Along with my little brother," Damon said drily.

With effort, Zara controlled her temper. She tended to see things from another angle entirely. It was a matter of record that the men in Damon's family were extremely good at seduction. Damon's uncle Tyler had swept Zara's mother off her feet; Damon had gotten Zara into bed in a matter of days. And now it seemed clear that Ben—who had routinely shambled into work around ten o'clock, taken long lunches and drifted away by four—had seduced poor Emily!

Zara moved on to another shelf of pamphlets, which was much nearer the front door, hoping Damon would take the hint. "As far as I'm concerned, Emily is outstandingly qualified and my best temp, and Ben has enticed her away. If anyone needs protection, it's Emily."

Damon gave Zara an incredulous look.

She checked her watch as if she was in a hurry to be somewhere. She had gotten seriously distracted by the Emily/Ben situation, but now she needed to wrap up the issue and get Damon out of her office before Rosie woke up. "I investigated Emily thoroughly before placing her on the books—she's perfectly trustworthy."

"Emily Harris is, but Emily Woodhouse-Harris isn't."

Zara froze as Damon slipped a folded sheet of paper out of his coat pocket and handed it to her. She stared at what was obviously a photocopy of a newspaper cutting depicting a more youthful Emily, the daughter of a disgraced financier who had lost all of his money, and that of the pension fund he had founded, in a financial crash. In the shot, Emily was dressed for the beach in a bikini and filmy sarong, and she was clinging to the arm of a prominent playboy businessman. One who, from the caption, had apparently dumped her in favor of marrying a socialite with her fortune intact.

Zara's jaw tightened. Her motto for Westlake Employment Agency was Reliable, High Quality, Vetted

Office Staff, Privacy and Discretion Guaranteed. In this case, the reliability part of the motto hadn't held. Neither had the privacy or the discretion.

However, the tacky little article, far from making Zara feel disappointed in Emily, only made her feel even more fiercely protective of an employee who reminded her an awful lot of herself. *Even down to the way Emily had lost everything and had been forced to invent a new life.* She knew exactly how Emily was going to feel when she saw the piece.

She set the incriminating article down on her desk. "You had Emily *investigated.*"

Damon's expression grew impatient. "I waited for you to call back. When you didn't, I made some calls of my own. As it turns out, I should have done it a whole lot earlier."

"Choosing to use one half of a double-barreled surname, and a previous relationship do not make Emily a bad risk!"

"Maybe not, but before Vitalis, Emily was involved with another wealthy businessman."

Now that she knew Emily's full name, the whole embarrassing scandal was coming back to her, which made her feel even sorrier for Emily. "From memory, the Woodhouse-Harrises moved in wealthy circles, so, of course, Emily would meet wealthy men."

"The relationships wouldn't be such a problem if Emily hadn't tried to conceal her past."

"Maybe she had good reasons for doing so."

Damon crossed his arms over his chest. "Such as?"

Zara's chin came up. She felt she was fighting on two fronts, for Emily and for herself. "For a start, it can't have been much fun having the media hounding her."

"Granted."

The curtness of his reply seemed to emphasize that the bottom line for Damon was Emily's so-called deception. "Emily happens to be very good at her job."

"I'm not disputing that, just her motives in seeking employment with wealthy men."

That touched a nerve, guiltily reminding Zara that if Damon found out her true identity, he would ascribe the same kind of gold-digging motivation to her. She doubted he would believe that it had been Zara's well-connected aunt who had set up the job interview and set her up by placing her back in Damon's orbit in the hope that she might score another cash offer. Or that Zara had zero interest in that money! "So you still think all Emily wanted was a wealthy husband?"

His expression cooled. "Or a lover. It's not exactly an uncommon motive."

His flat statement once again dredged up the stark memory of the legal letter she had received from Damon's lawyers. They'd offered to pay her off so she would not go to the press, attempt to contact his family or get her sticky fingers on the family inheritance. *As if.*

Zara could feel her blood pressure shooting through the roof. Before that moment, she had been able to separate Damon from the contents of that insulting letter, even though she knew he was the one who had authorized it. But now she realized how naive she had been. Damon's contempt for her and Petra was not so different from his ruthless assessment of Emily.

"There are women who don't give a hoot about your family's money, and Emily is one of them. She is not predatory."

A faint rustling sound from the interview room, as if Rosie was struggling out of her cozy blanket, sent a fresh surge of adrenaline shooting through Zara's veins. Damon's cool gaze fixed on the door, reminding her that not only did he possess exceptional eyesight, but that his hearing was no doubt excellent, as well. Attributes that, along with an uncanny sixth sense had, apparently, made him some kind of superspy during his time in the Special Forces. She needed to get Damon out of her office, now.

She forced a professional smile and apologized, which was more difficult than she expected. Bleakly, she realized she was still surprisingly angry with Damon. Although, she didn't know quite why that should be, since she was the one who had left Damon and not the other way around. Plus, she was *over* him, and had been for months.

She directed another breezy smile in Damon's general direction. As much as she thought Ben was at fault, it was clear the responsibility for the employment part of this disaster belonged with her. Damon's firm paid her to supply Magnum with the temping services they required, so it was up to her to fulfill the contract. She needed to find someone else to fill Emily's position, and fast, before Magnum took their business elsewhere.

"As luck would have it, I've got a temp on the books who might do to replace Emily. She's a little older, but extremely efficient—"

"No."

Zara blinked and plowed on. "Harriet has a long work record and an extremely good skill set—"

"I don't want Harriet," he said in a flat, cool voice. "I want you."

A pang of heat shot clear to Zara's toes, despite the fact that she knew Damon could only be referring to his need for an assistant. Even so, memories flickered, vivid and earthy, drawing every muscle of her body tight. She swallowed against a coiling tension that should not exist and desperately willed her body to return to normal. "Why?"

Damon's darkened gaze locked with hers for a piercing moment, and the reason she'd succumbed to a wild, irresponsible fling with him when she had known it was a huge mistake to sleep with the boss was suddenly crystal clear: chemistry. It shimmered in the air and ran through her veins like liquid fire, the pressure of it banding her chest, making it hard to breathe. For some unknown reason Damon had wanted her and, against all common sense, she had wanted him too.

Damon frowned and dragged lean fingers through

his hair and she received the indelible impression that for a long, stretched-out moment he had actually forgotten what he was going to say. "Uh, the McCall takeover. Before you disappeared, you did a lot of the groundwork—"

She stiffened at the mention of the McCall takeover. McCall Electrical being the company that had belonged to Tyler McCall. If there was ever a project she did not want to work on, it would be that one!

"I didn't disappear—I resigned without notice." *Then* she had disappeared. She'd had to get out of town quickly, because she had known that if she had tried to have a normal, aboveboard relationship with Damon, the press would have become interested in her. Even though they had no clue what Angel Atrides looked like, it would only have been a matter of time before her true identity was uncovered, then all the careful work she had done to invent a normal life and career would have been for nothing.

"Resignation?" he muttered in a low growl. "You sent a text."

Warmth rose in her cheeks. "But I did resign."

She knew she shouldn't belabor the point, but a combination of her anxiety over Damon walking into her office and her extreme physical response to him were having a bad effect on her. She couldn't seem to stop arguing with him, which was counterproductive. She needed to concentrate on getting rid of him before Rosie woke up.

Swallowing the exhilarating desire to argue some more, she reached for calm. "I agree that texting was not the ideal way to finish." It had just been necessary at the time, because she had not wanted Damon to have her private email address. Email addresses opened too many online doors, some of which led back to her old life, and she knew how adept Damon was at utilizing those sorts of opportunities.

Damon's thoughtful gaze seemed to burn right through her. "Whatever. Before you *left* without any notice or forwarding address, you did the groundwork for the McCall takeover. Despite a hitch in the proceedings, I'm now on the point of closing the deal, so I would prefer to have someone who knows their way around the issues."

Zara had the sudden, suffocating sense of being entangled in a sticky web from which she could not escape. "I had thought you would have completed that months ago."

"There's been an unexpected complication, a missing block of voters' shares that could jeopardize the takeover. And I've had…other things that have needed attention."

A picture of the gorgeous blonde he'd been dating lately, heiress to a media empire, Caroline Grant, flashed into Zara's mind. That image was instantly followed by a snapshot of the reed-slim redhead he had started seeing on a regular basis not long after Zara had left. Another hot dart of anger unsettled her further.

She did not want to admit that the anger could be linked with the fact that Damon had started dating less than a month after she left his bed. Wining and dining beautiful women while she had been hiding out in her aunt's country cottage, feeling exhausted and nauseous in the first trimester of her pregnancy. Because, if she was angry, that meant Damon was still important to her, or worse, that she was jealous.

Another small sound drew Damon's attention back to the door of the interview room. Zara's heart rate increased another notch. Rosie was definitely awake.

The vibration of a cell, thankfully, distracted Damon. Despite her clear need to get rid of Damon fast, a sudden intense curiosity manifested itself as he extracted the phone from his coat pocket and checked the screen.

Jaw taut, she watched as he slipped the phone back into his pocket. She wondered if the call had been from Caroline Grant, and suddenly her mind was made up.

"No. Working for you is out of the question, I have—"

"I realize you have a business to run," Damon cut in smoothly. "But I only need you for three weeks, four at most, until the negotiations are completed. And you do have a part-time assistant who could fill in for you."

Damon offered a fee that was so generous it would cover her agency costs for the next year. More, she would finally be able to afford to fly to Medinos to check out a mysterious safe-deposit box she had recently discovered her mother had obtained not long before she died.

But, as tempting as the money was, as much as she needed it, she could not risk being that close to Damon. As it was, she was kicking herself that she had allowed financial desperation to hold sway when she had accepted him as a client.

"I'm sorry. I can't work for you."

Walking briskly to her front door, she yanked it open. She had to get Damon out of her office before he discovered Rosie. He would take one look at her coalblack hair and eyes that were changing by the day to look eerily like his and would instantly know she was his daughter.

Cold, damp air flowed in, making Zara shiver, but instead of taking the hint and walking through the door, Damon paused and she made the fatal mistake of looking into his eyes.

Long, tense seconds later, Damon's gaze dropped to her mouth and the heady tension she had so far failed to control tightened another notch.

"Damn," he muttered, "I promised myself I wasn't going to do this."

Zara froze as he cupped her jaw, unwillingly riveted by the tingling heat that radiated out from that one point of contact, the unbearably familiar masculine scents of soap and skin. Despite the cold air, she could feel herself growing warmer by the second. Damon's touch was featherlight; all she needed to do was step away, so why couldn't she do that one simple thing?

It was a bad time to discover that, despite everything

that had happened, the heady excitement that had been her downfall a year ago was still just as potent, just as seductive.

It shouldn't be, she thought a little desperately. She had changed; she had moved on. When she did decide to allow a man back into her life it would not be because of an off-the-register sexual attraction. This time she would choose carefully. She needed steady and reliable, not—

Damon's mouth slanted across hers and any idea that the day was cold was blasted away by a torrent of heat. Her heart pounded so hard she found it difficult to breathe and her legs suddenly felt as limp as noodles.

This was why she had made "the mistake," she thought dimly. Her palms slid up over Damon's chest; her fingers convulsively gripped the lapels of his coat, as a familiar, guilty pleasure flooded her. Damon's hands settled at her waist, molding her more firmly against him and she found herself responding with an automatic, mindless pleasure, lifting up on her toes as she pressed into the kiss, clutching at his shoulders as if she couldn't get enough of him.

It was moth-to-the-flame stuff, irresistible and utterly dangerous, because it was abruptly clear to her that Damon was nothing short of an intoxicating addiction. When he was in the room she couldn't think; worse, she didn't want to think. As emancipated and independent as she was, as determined as she was to run her life in a practical, logical way, she had never been able to resist him.

Long, drugging seconds later Damon lifted his head. "Before I go, I have one more question."

A thin, high cry pierced the air. Zara's stomach sank. With a convulsive movement, she released her grip on Damon's coat.

Damon's gaze turned wintry. "Question answered."

With a sense of fatalism, undergirded by the sudden wrenching suspicion that Damon had known all along that there was a baby, Zara watched as he reached the door to the interview room in two gliding strides and pushed the door open wide.

Four

Damon stared at the baby in the bassinet.

He thought he had been prepared for this moment, but the reality of the tiny baby literally flipped his world upside down in the space of a moment.

The first thing he noticed about the child, *his child*, was the color of her sleep suit. Pink.

The tension banding his chest increased exponentially. Not only did he have a baby, he had a daughter.

"What's her name?" His voice came out more roughly than he cared for, but then it wasn't every day he discovered he was a father.

Emotion, painful and inchoate, seemed to burst through some interior barrier. With it came a torrent of memories. Memories that should have faded, but hadn't:

his father's voice late at night, the muffled sounds that meant his mother was being hit and was trying to stay quiet so he wouldn't know. Later, when he was older, the breathless pain of broken ribs, the harsh chemical scents of the hospital emergency room.

Once, a memory of reckless fury bursting through him when his father had attacked Damon's mother, who had been pregnant with Ben at the time. Ten years old, but big for his age, Damon had hit out and caught Guy Smith by surprise. He could still remember the rage behind that punch, the hot rush of satisfaction that had poured through him when his father had gone down.

Fatherhood, he thought bleakly. It was something he had consciously avoided, just as he avoided emotional relationships in general. As a child he had learned that the kind of intense out-of-control love most people seemed to wish for was neither a practical nor a safe basis for any relationship. Although, looking at the tiny baby whose gaze had latched onto his with singleminded intensity as she sucked on one small fist, he registered that you could not prove that by him. The first night he had spent with Zara had been characterized by a distinct lack of control.

He noted the fact that Zara was hovering at the door. "She's mine."

"Yes."

"And you didn't tell me, because…?"

Her gaze met his squarely before falling away. "It's… complicated." Her gaze homed in on his again, brows jerked together in a frown. "How did you find out? Let me guess... Emily?"

"Ben. When he phoned from the airport, he let it slip." Damon's jaw tightened. "He thought I already knew—"

"But if you'd known, we would have had this conversation a long time ago."

Damon tensed against the waft of a familiar flowery perfume as Zara brushed by him and slung a piece of muslin over one shoulder, presumably in case of spills. Picking the baby up with unconsciously graceful movements, she cuddled the infant close, Zara's expression softening in a way that briefly riveted him and, out of nowhere, desire kicked. Jaw tight, he registered the stubborn, visceral need to reclaim Zara, which should have evaporated in the instant he had uncovered the baby and her deception, and yet it hadn't.

In a moment of self-knowledge, he noted that it was tied to the fact that Zara was now the mother of his child and therefore qualified for his protection and support. As strong and independent as Zara seemed, he could no more abandon her and the baby than he had been able to step away from his own mother when she had been the victim of his father's abusive nature.

Added to that, as much as he had tried to intellectualize the process, the fact that Zara had given birth to his child had tipped some internal balance. He had felt the change in the instant that Ben had told him there was a baby. The primitive, testosterone-fueled desire that had gripped him to claim not just his child, but Zara too.

He watched as Zara rubbed the baby's back and he waited for more unwelcome memories of his childhood to surface and douse a need he didn't want. The memories didn't come. Probably, he thought bleakly, because his only memories of a baby in the family were of Ben. And by the time Ben was born their father had been dead and buried.

Damon began noticing other things in the room. A desk, which held what looked like Zara's handbag and, beside it, a newspaper and a small pile of mail. There were also a couple of chairs, and a large bag in one corner that seemed jam-packed full of baby things. Feeling suddenly overwarm, he shrugged out of his coat and dropped it over the back of a chair.

"Were you ever going to tell me?"

Her gaze flashed to his as, one-handed, she rummaged through the baby bag and extracted an insulated container holding a bottle of what he guessed was baby formula. "I didn't think, given that I was just an employee and that we'd had an office affair, that you would want to be tied to me by a chil—"

"It wasn't an affair."

"It was temporary."

Damon frowned at her clipped reply. He was still processing the fact that there really was a baby, but he was clear on one point. "Temporary or not doesn't change a thing. She's my child. I had a right to know."

And in the saying of it, he felt a further internal shift, the forging of a link that was irrevocable. It quietly but absolutely changed everything.

Zara's expression was taut as she settled the baby in her lap and coaxed her to accept the bottle. "You don't want children—you made no secret about that. I came across a magazine article where your wife claimed the reason your marriage broke up was that you didn't want children. She wasn't exactly reticent about the subject."

Damon frowned, irritated, despite the fact that for once the media was accurate. "That was true enough. Lily and I had an…arrangement—"

"As I remember it, so did we. A short-term liaison, no strings." She sent him the kind of crisp, business-like glance that assured him everything was settled.

Unfortunately, the slick managerial technique—straight out of Business Troubleshooting 101—only increased the fascination that had gripped Damon from the very first time he had met Zara. Over the years he had become used to being pursued by beautiful, successful women. With Zara, the opposite had proven to be true. And despite the clear evidence that she wanted him, she still seemed intent on avoiding him.

He should have been pleased. It was permission to step back, to keep his emotional involvement to a minimum, to simply be a biological father with legal access. No messy emotion or fallout when it all came apart.

The problem was, he thought grimly, that just minutes ago, Zara hadn't just let him kiss her, she had kissed him back. Despite walking out on him a year ago, she still wanted him. The mix of attraction and avoidance had an interesting but frustrating effect, fueling his need to have her back.

With every minute that passed, the desire to understand why Zara had run when she still clearly wanted him intensified. She had said she didn't want him to think she was after his money, and that she knew he didn't want children. Both were valid reasons, *if* their physical attraction had cooled off. But clearly it hadn't, which left him with a question mark.

"What's her name?"

The front door chime sounded.

Distracted, Zara peered past him into the office. "Rosamund, Rosie for short." She looked briefly torn. "Will you hold her while she finishes her bottle?"

A split second later, Zara was close enough that he could smell the flowery scent of her hair and other scents: the sourness of the milk spill on the muslin over her shoulder, the soft sweetness of baby powder.

"Hold her so her head is supported on your arm."

Damon froze as he found himself awkwardly cradling his daughter.

Zara handed him the bottle of formula, her expression both anxious and imperious. "Don't hold her so loosely. Closer, like this…"

She readjusted his hold so Rosie was cradled closer against his chest, her head resting comfortably in the crook of his arm. "And tilt the bottle—like this—so she doesn't gulp air."

Seconds later, Zara stepped out into the main office, closing the door firmly behind her.

Fumbling with the soft, warm bundle that wriggled and moved, Damon took the chair Zara had vacated and touched the nipple of the bottle to Rosie's lips. His anxiety that he was doing it all wrong evaporated almost instantly as Rosie's small hands clamped either side of the bottle and she began to drain what was left of the milk. After a minute or so the nipple popped out of her mouth, signaling that she was done. She stared at him unblinkingly, then put her fist into her mouth.

Gently, he attempted to lift her fist away and succeeded long enough that he caught a pearly flash against the redness of her gum before she was once again sucking on her fist. Feeling out of his depth, Damon let her have her way. If it was her fist that made her happy, who was he to argue?

Setting the bottle down on the desk, he eased himself into a more comfortable position and simply looked at the tiny warm creature in his arms. Something about Rosie informed him that even if she hadn't been wearing pink, he would have known she was a girl. It wasn't just that her skin was like porcelain and her features delicate— he guessed all babies shared those in common. And it wasn't the shock of silky dark hair that already showed a trace of curl, just like her mother's. Rather it was an indefinable, faintly imperious quality that announced her femininity, a quality her mother had in spades.

He dragged at his tie, loosening it. Rosie's gaze followed his action before she once more returned to a study of his face as if she was intent on imprinting his features. Caught in the net of his daughter's gaze, a profound sense of recognition riveted Damon. If there had been any doubt that he was Rosie's father, those doubts would have been nixed in that moment. Zara's eyes were a deep sapphire blue; Rosie's were already lightening to the unusual silvery gray that had run in his family for generations.

She had his eyes.

Something weird happened in the region of Damon's chest. He reached out a lean finger to touch a silky wisp of hair. Petal-soft fingers closed around his finger with surprising strength.

Rosie stared into his eyes, her gaze direct and fearless and, suddenly, she was her mother's daughter. Pale, delicate skin flushed and for a moment he thought she would cry. Instead her mouth curved in a gummy smile and he logged the moment that he fell utterly and completely under his daughter's spell.

"This complicates things," he muttered. "I'm not fit to be anyone's dad."

Rosie made a cute cooing sound. He tried to free his finger from her fierce grip, then was completely fascinated when she refused to let go.

"Babies have surprising strength." Zara's quiet voice broke his intense focus on his daughter.

He watched as she picked up the length of muslin, which had fallen to the floor, and briskly tucked it away in the baby bag, the movement jerky. "What's wrong?"

"Nothing! At least I hope it's nothing. But that was not the normal type of client that strolls in off the street. She was too well dressed, too pushy and she seemed more interested in the fact that you were seen walking in here than in applying for a job. I'm pretty sure she was a reporter of some kind."

Damon frowned. Normally the press didn't bother him too much. But that was because he usually made damn sure he wasn't in the public eye. For the past few months, however, he'd had an uncomfortable amount of exposure, because his current date, Caroline, championed a number of charities and had insisted on dragging him along to some high-profile events. As a result, he'd had one reporter in particular dogging his footsteps, trying to snag some kind of exclusive on his personal life.

"Was she blonde, thin, with red-rimmed glasses?"

Zara looked up from jamming the empty bottle into the baby bag, her expression arrested. "You *know* her?"

"Not exactly. She's a friend of Caroline's. She usually covers charity events."

"Caroline?" Zara zipped the bag closed with unnecessary force. "That would be your current girlfriend, which would make Red Glasses what? A gossip columnist?"

Now distinctly irritated, Damon rose to his feet. The motion seemed to distract Rosie, because she finally let go of his finger. "If we're talking about the same person, then her name's Vanessa Gardiner. She freelances for the tabloids and a couple of women's magazines."

He knew that because he had seen her parked outside his apartment a couple of times and just last week she had followed him to an exclusive restaurant where he'd had a client lunch. The intrusion had ticked him off to the point that he had tasked Walter, his head of security, with calling her off. Apparently, the tactic hadn't worked.

"So, she followed you here, to *my* employment agency? Why on earth would she want to do that?"

Damon worked to release the sudden tension in his jaw. Lately, it felt like he'd landed in the middle of a soap opera. At times like this, he missed the simplicity of the life in the military he had been forced to relinquish when he took over the family business. Chain of command was clear-cut and logical, unlike personal relationships.

"A few days ago, at an awards dinner, Caroline accused me of seeing someone else. Unfortunately, Gardiner must have been close enough to pick up on the conversation."

Zara straightened, her eyes shooting blue fire. "And are you seeing someone else?"

Damon got the sudden, arresting notion that if he'd said yes to Zara's snapped-out question she would have done something interestingly violent, like throw something at him. An odd, warm glow spread through him. "I'm not exactly in the habit of dating two women at the same time. Besides, you know my work schedule."

She blinked as if she was still having trouble controlling her emotions. "So this reporter is stalking you, trying to find evidence that there's another woman and she ends up in *my* office, where there's not only another woman, but a baby, as well!" Zara drew a deep breath. "Just what I need in my life right now."

Dragging a trailing tendril of hair behind one ear, she began to pace, even though there was very little room for pacing. "You should have called me before showing up—"

"I did. You didn't return my call."

Zara stared at him, frustrated. "What I don't get is why you want to be involved with Rosie or with me! From all accounts, it didn't take you long to get over me. Within a month you were dating that redhead. What was her name? Janet, Jessica—"

"Jemima."

She glared at him. "Whatever. Now you're dating Caroline and her little reporter friend is following you."

The silence in the small room stretched out, fraught and intense. Somewhere in the distance a car horn honked. The gusting wind was now laced by rain, which pattered on a barred window. It was an odd moment to discover one salient fact that somehow changed everything: Zara had been jealous of Jemima. And if Damon didn't miss his guess, she was jealous of Caroline.

Out of nowhere, his pulse rate lifted. Dealing with Zara was like trying to get information from a sphinx on lockdown. In normal conversation she was guarded and controlled. The only chink in her armor was that she hadn't yet learned to control her emotions or her body language.

Just minutes ago, she had kissed him. The memory of it still made every muscle in his body tighten. Now her eyes were shooting fire and she was making no bones about the fact that she didn't like it that he dated other women. Against all the odds, Zara's unguarded response settled something in him, a question that had remained unanswered for the past year. He didn't know why she had left him, but he was now certain it had not been because she didn't want him.

Feeling oddly buoyed, he cradled a now-sleepy Rosie a little closer and walked the few paces to the window, which looked out over a service lane. The rain had gotten heavier and the temperature in the room had dropped a couple of degrees. He made a mental note to ensure Zara and Rosie had adequate heating. "So, when did you discover you were pregnant?"

"A few days before I left."

That explained a few things: Zara had had a sick day when she had not seemed to be ill; her suddenly crammed schedule when, from the time they had started sleeping together, they had seldom spent a night apart.

His jaw tightened as memories he thought he had jettisoned came crowding back. He had to keep reminding himself that their relationship, such as it was, had lasted barely four weeks.

"I thought something had happened to you."

Until he had gone to her apartment and discovered that Zara had systematically packed up and left town. A quick word with the manager of the building had supplied the information that Zara had given notice some days before, which indicated the move had been carefully planned. "You could have talked to me. We could have worked something out."

Zara sent him a cool glance, left the room and returned almost immediately with the newspaper he had brought. She held it so that Ben and Emily's picture and the insulting headline were clearly visible. "Like this?"

"I'm not Ben."

"No, you're way more newsworthy. The media would have cut me to shreds. They would have made my life a misery." She tossed the newspaper into the trash can to one side of the desk.

Damon's gaze narrowed at the extremity of her reaction to the kind of publicity that was literally a five-minute wonder. He adjusted his hold on Rosie. "I could have arranged financial support."

Zara's head came up. "Money. Why did I know that it would come back to that? Do you always use money to solve your 'problems'?" She sketched quotation marks in the air.

He frowned at her reaction. "Not always. Sometimes a conversation works."

The phone ringing out in the office broke a tension that was suddenly thick enough to cut. There was an audible click as the call went through to the answering service.

"News flash," she said curtly. "With regard to your money, I don't want it. That's why I'm in business—I like to earn my own way."

Her glance was laced with defiance. With the flush on her cheeks and glossy tendrils of hair curling around her cheekbones, he couldn't help thinking that despite the buttoned-down suit and the attempt to tame her hair, Zara looked exotic and tempestuous.

Her flat statement underlined the certainty that had grown in him as he had cradled Rosie. He had thought that if there really was a child he would be able to control what he felt, that he could preserve his distance, but that idea had crashed and burned the second Rosie smiled at him.

One gummy smile and suddenly he had a whole new priority list.

He still intended to retrieve Ben ASAP, but, for the moment, Rosie and the attraction that was still very much alive between him and Zara had taken precedence over Ben and Emily's departure.

The implications were dizzying. After years of managing all his relationships, he was faced with two relationships that were distinctly out of his control. He should be drawing back, looking for ways to lessen his involvement and neutralize his dangerous emotions. The only trouble was, this time he didn't want to pull back. After years of being out in the cold, he couldn't seem to resist the warmth.

Damon glanced down at Rosie, who had dropped off to sleep in his arms with a relaxed abandon that was mesmerizing. Her cheeks were delicately flushed, her lashes dark, silky crescents against her skin. For a moment, he was transfixed by the phenomenon, which had at its heart the absolute trust a child gave to a parent. The kind of trust he had never thought would be given to him, but which now seemed vital.

He felt the moment of decision, a quiet settling into place of a plan that, less than an hour ago, would have been out of the question. A plan that would include both Rosie and Zara in his life.

The risk of attempting such a thing registered, but the concept of that risk was almost instantly swamped by a surge of possessiveness.

There was no reason he couldn't successfully incorporate Zara and Rosie into his life. But he had to be careful. Zara had walked away from him once before, disappearing almost without trace; he could not afford for that to happen again. This time he would move more slowly and the way forward seemed clear.

"Okay, let's talk business. Now that Emily's gone, I need a PA."

The wariness disappeared from Zara's expression

with fascinating speed as she shifted into business mode. "I have a couple more possibilities on the books," she said smoothly. "A retired accountant who is looking for part-time work—although I'm sure he'd be happy to fill in for Emily for a couple of weeks. And a researcher who will probably be perfect—"

"Like I said before," Damon said flatly. "I don't want the temps on your books. We're out of time and you've worked on the takeover. I want you."

Shock reverberated through Zara at the flat demand of the last three words.

Even though Damon had couched the barely concealed demand in business terms, for a sharp, visceral moment Zara still registered that he wanted *her*. Not good.

She took a deep breath, which she suddenly desperately needed. The chemistry thing was happening again. Her heart was beating too fast and her skin felt oddly sensitive, her breasts taut. In certain places there was a distressing, tingling heat that was all too familiar...

She crossed her arms over her chest and tried to get a grip on herself. Because this was the same craziness that had gotten her into trouble in the first place. "I'm not available."

"If you're worried about this office, I'll compensate you for the cost of increasing Molly's hours, or even employing someone to replace you while you work for me. I'm also happy to pay for childcare. In fact, *all* of Rosie's childcare."

He glanced around the small room, which normally Zara barely registered, but she was noticing it now. Aside from Rosie's clutter, there was just the cheap desk and two chairs. Even the carpet, which was gray and threadbare in places, highlighted the fact that she had run out of money when it came to this room. The small decor budget she'd allowed herself had all been expended on the front office, because first impressions counted.

Damon's gaze pinned her. "This isn't charity—it's a business proposition."

Zara drew a swift breath. Damon's offer shouldn't have flicked her on the raw, but it did, since the last time Damon had offered her money it had been so she would go away for good. Not that he knew that!

"Like I said before, I really don't want your money."

"But you need it."

Shock jerked through her at the flat certainty in his voice, as if he knew just how financially stretched she was. Panic gripped her, making it hard to breathe. "You've been investigating me."

She didn't know why she hadn't thought of that before. Damon was in the surveillance business after all and she had read enough about Magnum to know that the company included a range of complementary businesses, one of them an actual detective agency.

Damon's gaze narrowed. "Believe it or not, I don't

make a practice of investigating the women I sleep with. I like to think I can step away from the paranoia of the security business and have something approaching a normal life outside work hours. The reason I know you need the money is that you agreed to take Magnum Security on as a client. Given your reluctance to even take a phone call from me, it was fairly easy to conclude that you needed the money."

Zara drew a deep breath and tried to calm down. She had always known that if Damon decided to put her life under a microscope, he would unravel her secrets fairly quickly. Logically, the fact that he hadn't turned up at her door until now meant that he hadn't. Even so…

"It's still got to be no when it comes to money," she said stiffly. "I can manage."

Damon frowned. "Whether you want my money or not, the second I declare my paternity and apply to pay child support, you'll receive it, anyway."

The words *declare paternity* and *child support* stopped Zara in her tracks. Damon declaring his paternity was a legal process, which would inevitably result in Rosie's birth certificate being updated to include his name. Then that document would be supplied to Damon. When Damon looked at the birth certificate he would see Zara's name change and that her mother had been Petra Atrides, aka Petra Hunt.

If that wasn't bad enough, when the tax agency assessed his income and began making her mandatory child support payments from his bank account, he would hate her even more. Originally, he had tried to get rid of Zara, aka Angel, with one cash payment; now he would be stuck with years of payments. And because Damon earned a great deal, those payments would be substantial.

Zara tried to think, but she felt like she was caught in a whirlwind. Now that he had discovered Rosie, those legal processes would happen. There was nothing she could do to stop them. The only thing she could do was angle for time while she tried to figure out how to tell Damon the truth about herself without forever damaging his relationship with Rosie. And how to make the money problem go away.

Suddenly the interview room seemed claustrophobically small. In need of air and a few seconds' respite so she could *think*, Zara opened the door and peered out into her office. It was empty, and thanks to the rain, the street outside was fairly deserted.

The reporter seemed to have disappeared. Although, Zara didn't think she had seen the last of Vanessa Gardiner. She had stared at Zara as if she was a hound dog on the scent. Zara had gotten the distinct impression that Vanessa knew Zara used to work for Damon and now she was busily putting two and two together. That meant Vanessa would be back, and if she saw Zara with Rosie, the game would be up.

Zara tried to shake the horribly familiar hunted feeling—the same feeling she'd experienced when the press had tracked her after Petra's death—but it wouldn't go away. Whether she was right or wrong, her instincts told her she needed to be absent from West-lake Employment for a while.

Right now, her only option seemed to be to work for Damon. It felt a little like jumping out of the frying pan into the fire, but it was a fact that Damon worked in a hermetically sealed, high-security environment, fourteen stories up. Even the underground parking area was private and secure. To all intents and purposes, unless Gardiner found out where Zara lived, she would have seemed to have disappeared off the face of the planet.

Turning back, she met Damon's gaze squarely. "I could work for you, but on the condition that I'll need to bring Rosie with me. If that reporter tracked you here and thinks we might be involved, then there's no way I'm risking having her find out about Rosie or tracking her to her day care center."

"Not a problem. If you want an alternative center, I have a friend who owns a childcare franchise."

He mentioned the name of an exclusive franchise that was way out of her price range. The only problem was, she didn't think any center was safe, at least for the moment. And the way the tabloids had jumped on the story about Ben and Emily was just a dress rehearsal for the way they would behave when they discovered Zara had given birth to Damon's child.

"I just don't want to risk the press finding out Rosie is yours until we've had time to…settle things."

Suddenly, needing to have her daughter close, Zara

held out her arms and was inordinately relieved when Damon instantly handed Rosie over. Unfortunately, in the process, Zara had to get closer to Damon than she liked. His arms brushed hers and his breath washed over one cheek. The intimacy of the contact sent another one of those sharp little pangs through her.

Damon shrugged out of his jacket, which had a small milky spill on it and picked up a container of baby wipes that resided on the desk. "Can I use one of these?"

She nodded and tried not to watch as Damon perched on the edge of the desk and dabbed at the stain. Suddenly, he seemed too large and too male for the tiny office, with the breadth of his shoulders stretching the cut of his jacket and the bronze color of his skin glowing through the white cotton of his shirt.

Feeling edgy and unsettled and still whirling from the decisions she'd had to make, Zara placed Rosie on one shoulder and gently rubbed her back, encouraging her daughter to stay asleep. Anything but dwell on the relaxed intimacy of Damon cleaning the stain from his jacket with Rosie's wipes—the kind of small, fascinating action that went with couplehood, or families.

He looked up, catching her off guard. "Rosie's teething, by the way. When she put her fist in her mouth her gums were red and I saw a glimpse of white."

Instantly distracted, Zara lowered Rosie into the bassinet. Gently, she examined her mouth and was stunned to see a tiny glimmer of white edging through Rosie's gum.

Three months was very early for teething, although

Zara had learned from another young mother whose baby had been born with tiny "milk teeth" that anything could happen. "You're right, it must have just come through. No wonder she's had trouble sleeping." She shot Damon a faintly chagrined look. "How did you know?"

"My ex-wife's sister had twins. They both teethed early."

Zara could feel herself stiffening at his easy mention of his ex-wife, Lily. Shortly after Zara had discovered who Damon really was, two weeks into her tempestuous six weeks with him, she had searched online for snippets about his gorgeous, blonde and seemingly perfect ex-wife. Lily had since married again to an extremely wealthy banker.

Lily and Damon had seemed to have a poster-perfect marriage, which had ended in a quick and quiet divorce a few years ago. Logically, Zara knew that all the talk about perfection had to be untrue, since Lily and Damon had divorced, but Zara's mood had plummeted, anyway. It had underlined her decision to leave without telling Damon she was pregnant. If Damon had not been satisfied with Lily, how on earth could he ever contemplate a real relationship with Zara?

Damon shrugged back into his jacket. Zara was caught and held by the way his shirt briefly stretched across his muscled chest, and the flood of intimate memories that sight evoked, most of which had to do with breathless heat and naked skin. Predictably, his gaze caught hers in that moment, but this time she managed to quickly look away, although she couldn't do a thing about the warmth that seared her cheeks.

A split second later, he closed the distance between them as he came to look down at Rosie. Zara was caught and held by the softness of his expression. It was a softness she had only ever seen in flashes, usually for the elderly or the very young.

"I'll let Howard know you're taking the job."

Her heart jolted at the singular clarity of Damon's gaze, the silvery irises with their dark striations, the thick, silky fringe of lashes. For a long, breathless moment her mind went completely blank. "Just so we're clear, I'll work for you for the time it takes to complete the McCall takeover, on the condition that your relationship to Rosie is kept secret until after the deal is completed."

Damon's incisive, wintry gaze settled on hers for an uncomfortable period of time, reminding her that when it came to deception she was a desperate amateur, while he had a formidable skill set. In terms of her deception she was suddenly profoundly aware that the clock was ticking.

He shot the cuff of his jacket and checked his watch, as if he needed to be somewhere. "Agreed. I've no more wish that the press get wind of this than you. I won't let on that Rosie is mine until the takeover is completed, and until after we've settled the custody arrangements."

Custody. Another crazy jolt to her heart. Implications

she hadn't thought of flooded her, such as the fact that Rosie now had two parents instead of one. Rosie was no longer solely Zara's. She was so used to having her soft, sweet daughter all to herself, of being a cozy, self-sufficient family of two, that it was hard to consider the changes that were coming.

She was quite sure Damon would never try to take Rosie from her. She was equally certain that he would be entirely reasonable in terms of custody. Even so, the notion of sharing Rosie shook Zara, underlining that her cut-and-dried, controllable life had just swung wildly off course.

Added to that, with the inescapable link of Rosie binding Zara to Damon, she no longer had the option of running and hiding. She would once more have to face the world as Petra Hunt's daughter.

The last woman in the world Damon would wish to be the mother of his child.

Five

Damon strolled down the windswept road in the direction of his Jeep Cherokee. His phone vibrated again. He ignored it, just like he'd ignored the last call, then grimaced as he saw his security chief camped out by Damon's Jeep, phone to his ear.

Walter, a retired assault specialist in the Special Forces, terminated his call. "You could have answered. I was worried. The whole office is in an uproar—"

"Can't see why." Damon found his car keys and unlocked the Jeep. "I was only gone for a couple of hours."

Walter tapped his watch. "Four hours. You missed two appointments, but don't worry, Howard rescheduled. He's more of a blunt instrument than a personal assistant, but he managed to quiet old man Sanderson down. Didn't have much success with Caroline though. Think you've got a bit of work to do there."

Damon went still. "You let Howard talk to Caroline?" Howard Prosser was another ex-army employee—an accountant and steely-eyed auditor who had routinely struck fear into entire military bases. Conversation was an art form that Howard had never mastered. Normally, he happily remained locked in his office and preferred communicating via email.

"It was more a succession of grunts than actual speech." Walter looked reflective. "I think he likes her."

Damon could feel a familiar frustration kicking in. Caroline Grant, the daughter of a real estate magnate, was elegant, beautiful and intelligent. She epitomized the qualities of the kind of woman he wanted to be attracted to, but unfortunately, that was where it ended. There was a vital component missing. Ever since his marriage to Lily had quietly imploded, Damon had become acutely aware of what that component was. As perfect as she was, he did not truly want Caroline.

The situation reminded him of his marriage. On the surface everything looked perfect, but there was a lack of spontaneity, of *warmth* that ruled out real intimacy. The problem was that Caroline, and almost every other woman he had dated aside from Zara, was just a little too much like him, more interested in a cool, carefully negotiated partnership than in flinging caution to the wind and plunging into a fiery, risky liaison.

He tensed as a vivid image of Zara, wrapping her

arms around his neck and lifting up on her toes to kiss him, momentarily blanked his mind and made every cell in his body tighten. The honking of a car as it braked behind a delivery truck dragged him back to the chilly gray present and the conversation with Walter.

"Uh, what did Caroline say?"

Walter reached into his pocket. "She left you a note."

Damon took and opened the note. A ticket fluttered to the pavement. He skimmed the neat, slanted writing, which was heavily indented into the page, as if Caroline had pressed quite hard with the pen as she wrote. The message was succinct. Since he had missed their discussion about his promise of support for her latest charity over lunch last week and canceled their lunch date today, she had taken the liberty of signing him up for the gala evening she had arranged that evening. He could pick her up at six, sharp.

Walter scooped up the ticket and handed it to him. "A ticket to a gala ball. You hate gala balls."

With passion. Damon slipped the ticket into his wallet.

Walter's brows jerked together. "I hope you're not getting maneuvered into anything serious here."

A grim smile quirked one corner of Damon's mouth. Walter had been around for his marriage breakup and was somewhat protective. "Don't worry. I've got a feeling Caroline and I are strictly short-term."

Caroline needed an escort for tonight, but from the brevity of the note and the depth of the indentations, even piercing the page on the final period, whatever it was they had shared was over.

"All I can say," Walter muttered, "is that this city lifestyle is a far cry from Afghanistan."

"You hated Afghanistan."

"Margot hated Afghanistan," Walter corrected. "If I wanted to save my marriage, something had to go. Turns out it was the job. By the way, pretty sure I saw Vanessa Gardiner driving away just as I got here."

Damon's gaze narrowed as he automatically skimmed the flow of traffic. "She tried to fool Zara into thinking she needed a job."

Walter's eyebrows shot up. "I'll bet that went well."

Damon climbed behind the wheel and nosed into traffic. He hadn't told Zara, but he was pretty sure it was Caroline who had manipulated the reporter into doing a little digging. She had become increasingly suspicious that there was another woman. For him, the suspicion spelled the end to a relationship that had grown increasingly irritating.

He was aware of Walter following close behind. Walter and Margot were longtime friends. There was nothing flashy or luxe about them. They had three kids, all grown now, and they lived a comfortable but low-key life. However, ordinary or not, they possessed something that had eluded Damon—a relationship that had lasted through thick and thin, characterized by warmth, loyalty and family values.

The fact that he was a father hit him anew.

He braked as traffic ahead slowed. He was still struggling to come to grips with the surge of possessiveness that had hit him out of left field for Rosie *and* Zara, and which was now driving a whole bunch of decisions that, twenty-four hours ago, would not have been viable.

Zara was making no bones about wanting to preserve her distance, which should have pleased him. After all, her reaction dovetailed with his own preference for avoiding emotional entanglements. Instead, contrarily, Zara's determination to remain independent had only served to aggravate and annoy him even more for one salient reason: he still wanted her.

His tactics in forcing Zara to work for him had been blunt and crude, but the situation was nonnegotiable. He was a father and that changed everything. He didn't just want to be a weekend visitor; he wanted Rosie in his life.

And, against all the odds, that was the way he was beginning to think about Zara too.

The lights changed. He accelerated into the inner city and took the ramp down into the parking garage beneath the gleaming office block that contained his offices and a penthouse apartment.

Damon held the private elevator for Walter, who had driven in directly behind him.

Walter grunted his thanks. As the elevator shot upward, Walter stared blandly at the floor numbers as they flashed. "What are you going to do about the baby?"

With a sense of resignation, Damon met Walter's

gaze. He tried to tell himself that if his head of security couldn't find out that kind of information he would have been disappointed. "You've spoken to Ben."

"First thing when he landed. He's worried about you."

The elevator doors glided open. Damon checked his watch as he stepped into the foyer of Magnum Security. By his calculation, Ben and Emily would have landed a couple of hours ago, right about when Damon had been walking the streets, looking for Zara's office.

Walter waited until they were in the privacy of his office before he fired his next question. "Don't tell me you're going to marry her."

Damon shrugged out of his coat and hung it on the hook behind the door. "With a child in the mix, maybe it's the logical solution."

Walter gave him the kind of polite stare that said he wasn't buying that for an instant. "There are other solutions."

Damon had thought of them all. He could simply arrange access, offer financial assistance and step out of the picture, job done.

The problem was, he thought broodingly, that Zara had kissed him. And it hadn't been just a kiss. There had been a fierceness to it that had riveted him.

"The baby changes things."

Walter frowned. "I don't see why you would even consider marriage. Zara's not exactly your usual type."

Damon's brows jerked together. "My usual type?"

Walter looked uncomfortable. "Classy, thin, *blonde*—"

"Instead of brunette, curvy, in charge." Despite the raft of problems involved with even attempting to have a relationship with Zara, Damon found himself grinning. "Favorite word, *no*."

There was a heavy silence. "So there's nothing I can say?"

"Relax, I'm not proposing a normal marriage." *With its inherent emotional instability.* "I'm talking about a marriage of convenience."

Walter's expression turned dour. "Seems to me I've heard those words before."

Right before Damon had married Lily. And there was his dilemma.

If a marriage of convenience hadn't worked with someone as sweet and straightforward as Lily, he was going to have his work cut out convincing a complicated career woman like Zara that it was the ideal solution.

On the plus side, he thought grimly, there would be no issues about whether or not to have children, because there was already a baby. Then there was the sex.

The thought of having Zara back in his bed made every muscle in his body lock up. He was abruptly aware of just how sexy and gorgeous Zara was, and that he had left her alone for over a year. In that time, he had to assume the only reason she hadn't gotten involved with another man had been because she was pregnant, then dealing with a new baby.

Damon stared out his window, barely noticing the

bustling marina below or the grey, scudding clouds. He felt like a sleeper waking up. Just over a year ago, he had convinced himself he needed to walk away from Zara, but in doing so he had left her alone and available. Now he was acutely aware that if he didn't lay claim to Zara ASAP, it was only a matter of time before some other man did.

And that was happening over his dead body.

Zara opened the door of her tiny rented house in Mount Eden, which had become her haven in the last few months, and carried Rosie, who was sleeping peacefully after the car ride, through to her room. Frowning a little at the damp chill of the house, Zara laid Rosie down in her cot and tucked a warm quilt around her before turning on the wall heater and tiptoeing out.

She walked back out to the garage, shivering in the chill of the evening as she retrieved her handbag from the car. Hooking the strap over one shoulder, she hefted the bulging baby bag, which was now mostly filled with dirty things that needed laundering and bottles that needed to be washed out. Locking the car, she walked back into the house, awkwardly flicking on lights as she went.

The comforting scent of the chicken casserole she had put into the slow cooker that morning made her mouth water and her stomach rumble. After Damon's disruptive visit, she'd been too unsettled to eat more than a few bites of the sandwich she had packed. Until that moment, she hadn't realized just how hungry she was.

With a sigh of relief, she dropped the bags onto a couch. As she straightened, she caught a disorienting flash of her reflection in the mirror over an antique drinks cabinet that had once belonged to her aunt. Apart from her hair wisping around her face and the color in her cheeks, she didn't look a lot different from that morning. The problem was she *felt* different, off balance and distinctly unsettled, as if a low-grade electric current was shimmering through her veins, making her heart beat faster and putting her subtly on edge.

And she knew exactly why that was. In the space of a few hours, everything had changed. Emily had run off with Ben; Damon had discovered Rosie; Zara was back working for Damon; that darned reporter had found her...and Zara had kissed Damon.

A sharp pang of awareness zapped through her at the memory of the heated, out-of-control kiss. She had tried to convince herself that it had been an experiment, that in kissing Damon she could somehow exorcise the craziness of their past attraction and put him firmly in his place: in the past. But the truth was, aside from acknowledging her own unwilling attraction to Damon, she had been blindsided by the fierceness of her own need and utterly seduced by the fact that *he* still wanted her.

Frowning at her instant and unwanted reaction just to the memory, Zara turned on the heater in the sitting room, then walked through to the kitchen. She lifted the lid on the slow cooker. The rich fragrance of the chicken filled her tiny kitchen. She switched the cooker off so that by the time she was ready to eat, the food would have cooled a little. She put water in the kettle, and when it boiled and the tea was made, she wrapped her fingers around the mug and sipped, enjoying the comfort and the warmth and the automatic cue to wind down and relax.

Her cell chimed. She carried the tea out to the sitting room, set it down on the coffee table and fished her phone out of her bag. She picked up the call, then stiffened as she registered an unfamiliar number.

The low timbre of Damon's voice made her clench her stomach.

"How did you get this number?"

"I needed to access some of Emily's email correspondence. I found your number listed in her contacts."

Zara's stomach sank. She should have seen this coming. Since Emily had actually resigned, of course Damon would have to retrieve correspondence and files from her computer, along with contact information.

"I'm sending a car for you and Rosie in the morning—"

"I don't need you to send a car. I have a car."

"That's hardly practical since you'll have to find parking and carry Rosie and all of her baby gear through the streets."

Zara stiffened. The fact that Damon now had a legitimate stake in Rosie's life was suddenly real and she couldn't help feeling a certain resistance to the idea. "It's not a problem—I can put Rosie in a front pack. She's light, and the bag isn't much heavier than—"

"This is purely a practical solution, designed to make things easier for you."

She tensed at the low, curt timbre of his voice. When she had first gone to work for Damon, before she had known exactly who he was, he had made a lot of things easier and much more enjoyable for her. Gorgeous working lunches, a car and driver for office errands or when she'd had to work late. There had even been a clothing allowance, which, of course, she had not spent on clothes but had put aside for a deposit on a house. And the problem was, that generosity hadn't been just for her. He had been generous to everyone, no matter their position in the firm. Working for Damon, and falling for him, had been heaven—until she had discovered he was Tyler McCall's nephew.

Zara forced herself to loosen her grip on the phone. She could not allow herself to dwell on the past or become emotional about things she could not change. It had been a stressful day; tomorrow would be even worse.

All she knew was that she had to lay down some ground rules, fast. She could not afford to be seduced by Damon's openhanded generosity. Especially since, once he knew who she was, he would regret ever employing her. He would regret sleeping with her.

"Thanks, but no thanks. I don't need you, or anyone, to make things easier for me."

There was a small silence. "I thought you wanted to keep Rosie under wraps. If you park somewhere in town and walk to the building, that won't be possible."

Her stomach sank. "I hadn't thought about that." She stared bleakly into space and tried to think. She hated to admit it, but Damon was right. Entering Damon's office building lugging a baby bag and carrying Rosie was too big a risk. "Okay."

There was a brief silence. "The car will be outside your house at eight thirty."

"I suppose you also know where I live?"

"Don't make it sound creepy. Emily didn't have that information, but there was mail on the desk in the interview room where Rosie was sleeping. Since the street address was different to your agency address, it didn't take a genius to figure out that was where you lived."

Her fingers tightened on the phone. In the panic of Damon discovering Rosie, she had completely forgotten that she had left some personal mail on the desk. At the time it had seemed an innocuous thing to do, because she hadn't imagined anyone but herself entering that particular interview room. And, somehow, over the past year she had forgotten what Damon had done for a living, that beneath the designer suit and white linen shirt were the kinds of scars that did not come from a tame city existence. That, as effective as he was in the boardroom, he had another far more formidable skill set.

A feminine voice, somewhere in the background, shattered the last illusory remnants of intimacy. Damon coolly requested that Zara give him a minute.

Zara knew she shouldn't continue to listen, that she should allow Damon a measure of privacy, but she couldn't help straining to pick up snatches of the muffled conversation and the name *Caroline*.

Zara jerked the phone from her ear. That would be Damon's beautiful, wealthy, current girlfriend.

The kind of woman who moved in Damon's circles and who the tabloids and magazines and social media forums uniformly pronounced had the perfect profile to be the next Mrs. Smith.

Zara's cheeks burned with a sudden bone-deep embarrassment as she remembered the way she had kissed Damon that morning. She had completely forgotten that he was dating Caroline.

Out of nowhere, gloom settled over her, which was annoying. She should be happy that Damon had moved on so quickly. It put the fling they had shared in perspective.

Suddenly done with the conversation and just a little panicked by her own response to Damon, she terminated the call. Her behavior was abrupt and rude, cutting Damon off midspeech, but she didn't care. Setting the phone down on the coffee table, Zara paced to the window and stared out at the cold, rain-spattered night. She felt horribly off balance, one minute vibrating with anger at Damon, the next with anger at herself for responding to him. The loss of control was worrying. She couldn't help thinking that the last time she'd lost control of her emotions, she had gotten pregnant.

Her stomach churned hollowly, reminding her that she still hadn't eaten, which was probably why she felt so emotional and vulnerable. She was suffering from a blood sugar low.

Walking to the kitchen, she ladled some of the casserole into a bowl, grabbed a fork, returned to the sitting room and curled up on the sofa. After saying grace, she turned on her small TV and ate the chicken. Despite her hunger, she barely tasted it. She even had trouble concentrating on her favorite show, which was all about couples buying their dream homes. It had an irresistible appeal for Zara, because ever since she and Petra had lost their pretty villa on Medinos, she'd longed for a home, something that wasn't possible with Petra's jet-setting lifestyle.

For most of the year, she had been away at boarding school. During vacations, Petra would fly Zara to some exotic location, often someone else's house, or a holiday villa Petra had rented for the summer.

Very occasionally, Zara had stayed with her aunt Phoebe, which she had actually adored because Phoebe's house had become the closest thing she'd had to a home. She had loved the "sameness" of Phoebe's old Victorian villa, even if it had involved heavy furniture and walls of dusty books. She had loved having the same room every time, and the same narrow single bed with the squeaky spring. Even the scents of the garden and the fragrant meadow beyond had somehow spelled home.

The show came to an end. Still tense and unsettled, Zara switched the TV off and sat for long minutes just enjoying the sound of rain pattering on the roof and the cozy ticking of the heater. Sounds that should have relaxed her, but which barely registered. Because beneath the anger and the nervy tension was a thread of awareness, a feminine response to Damon, that shouldn't have been there.

Thoroughly annoyed with herself, she carried her bowl and fork back to the kitchen and rinsed them. If she was going to get through these next few weeks, she needed to get her head straight. It was a chance to sort out the future in a way that was acceptable to them both. A chance to earn money that would help her achieve the dream of her own home. A chance to afford the trip to Medinos to retrieve her mother's safe-deposit box.

Zara stopped, a damp tea towel in her hand, as the possibility of a future with some measure of financial security opened up. She did not want to be all about money, but with Rosie in the picture, she had to be.

The safe-deposit box could change everything for her and Rosie.

Zara had discovered that there was a safe-deposit box when her cousin Lena had given her a packet of letters that had been stored in Aunt Phoebe's house. Phoebe had died several months ago, but it hadn't been until recently that Lena, who lived in Australia, had been able to clean out the house and put it up for sale. When she'd cleaned out her mother's desk, she'd found the letters Zara's mother had sent to Phoebe over the years.

One evening, a couple of weeks ago, Zara had finally read through them. The hairs at the back of her neck had stood on end when she had read the final letter her mother had written, which mentioned that she had decided to get a safe-deposit box after a string of burglaries near the apartment she had rented. When Phoebe received the letter, she had been hospitalized, so, understandably, she had never mentioned the possibility to Zara.

After learning of the box, Zara had searched through her mother's effects, which she had stored in her spare room. She had finally found a small tagged key with the address of her mother's bank on Medinos.

Her knees wobbly, Zara had sat on the edge of her bed, staring at the key, a tingle electrifying her spine. Petra had always said she would look after Zara, that she had an investment plan. Zara had taken that to mean that her mother had invested with some financial institution or had deposits at her bank, but nothing of the sort had ever come to light.

Petra had, at times, made a great deal of money and she had also possessed some expensive pieces of jewelry that had vanished. Petra could have sold the jewelry to supplement her income as her career tailed off. However, a safe-deposit box suggested otherwise.

With any luck, there might be items of sufficient value to put a deposit down on a house. It was also possible that Zara's Atrides grandmother's jewelry, which had been missing from Petra's personal things, might also be in the box.

Zara did not know if the Atrides jewelry was valuable or not. The important thing was that pieces had been handed down the family line. They were her last tangible link to her father's family, aside from the name itself and a defunct title, both of which she did not use.

The safe-deposit box could be an Aladdin's cave of jewelry that would restore her grandmother's pieces to her, with the addition of enough soulless diamonds to fund a house. Then again, it could contain a disappointing array of trinkets that would not cover the cost of the airfare.

When she completed this temping job with Damon, she would finally be in a position to find out.

She finished drying the dishes, then divided up the remaining casserole, which was enough to make several meals, into containers. Once they were labeled and dated, she stacked them in her small freezer, then moved on to sorting through Rosie's bag, disposing of rubbish and putting soiled things into the laundry. Zara finished by washing Rosie's bottles and repacking the bag with formula, fresh diapers and the one hundred other things a baby seemed to need.

Feeling much calmer and more in control, Zara quickly showered and changed into leggings and a soft T-shirt. Shivering at the chill in her bedroom, she also pulled on a thick sweater.

Combing her hair out and leaving it to dry naturally, she padded back to the kitchen. She caught a glimpse of her reflection in the window over the bench. Not for the first time she was confronted by the fact that, with her dark hair and curvy figure, she was starkly different from the elegant blondes Damon seemed attracted to.

Caroline was a case in point. She was classically beautiful and stylish, a virtual carbon copy of Damon's ex-wife, Lily. The similarities reaffirmed that Zara was the exact opposite of the kind of woman he clearly preferred.

Which begged the question, why had he slept with her in the first place?

Feeling annoyed with herself for falling into the trap of comparing herself with other women who had nothing whatsoever to do with her life—unless one of them became Rosie's stepmother, and she didn't want to think about that—Zara found her laptop. Sitting down on the couch, she flipped it open. Usually she checked in with a few friends on social media or read a downloaded book until she felt sleepy, but on impulse, she typed Caroline's name into a popular search engine.

A huge selection of hits appeared. At the top of the list was a video feed of a charity dinner that had been posted less than thirty minutes before.

Stomach tight, knowing she shouldn't do it but unable to resist, she hit the play button. Her screen filled with an image of Caroline in a sexy pale peach gown with a plunging neckline and a slit that revealed one slender, perfectly tanned leg. According to the commentary, normally, Caroline preferred her blonde hair up, but tonight she had opted for a more natural look, and had styled her hair smooth and straight so that it flowed silkily around her shoulders. The reason? Her soon-to-be fiancé, Damon Smith.

Zara stabbed the pause button, but she was too late. The screen froze on a shot of Caroline, one arm coiled around a dark sleeve as Damon, looking broodingly masculine in a tux, half turned to end up center shot.

Her chest tight and burning with an emotion she did not want to label, Zara wondered if she was actually going to be sick.

Suddenly, the dilemma of accepting a lift to work, even with the risk of a nosy reporter, was decided. She would rather die than get into one of Damon's fabulous, glossy company cars. If Damon's driver was parked outside her house at eight thirty, then he would have a wasted trip, because she would be gone by eight.

She dragged in one breath, then another. Dimly, she registered a piece of knowledge that she had avoided for some time through the simple tactic of refusing to think about it, period.

She was jealous of Caroline. And there was nothing either gentle or half-hearted about the emotion, which pulsed through Zara in fiery waves. She had been jealous for months, ever since she had read on a social media site that Damon had started dating the blonde.

Jumping to her feet, Zara began to pace. Just seconds ago, she had felt tired, maybe even a little depressed. Now restless energy hummed through her.

Damon was going to marry Caroline.

How could he? When he had just found out he had fathered a child? *Their* child.

Clearly, Rosie did not mean as much to him as he had implied today. Although, unpalatably, it wasn't Damon's relationship with his daughter that was upsetting her so badly. It was his utter lack of a relationship with *her*.

The reason she was jealous of Caroline was blazingly simple. It had been staring her in the face for weeks, but she had been too intent on burying her head, and her emotions, in the sand.

She still wanted Damon.

Six

Zara ended up at one end of her tiny sitting room, staring at the rain streaming down her window. Feeling like an automaton, she jerked the curtains together, closing out the night.

Blankly, she forced herself to face the fact that Damon and Caroline were soon to be engaged. And why not? They had been dating for months. It should not have come as a shock.

But it had, she thought grimly, especially after the kiss they'd shared.

Numbly, she moved to the small set of French doors that opened out onto a drenched patio and yanked a second set of curtains closed. The fact was, the kiss had stirred up feelings she had thought she had suppressed, making her feel intimately, possessively connected with Damon, as if he was still her lover. And now Caroline had taken him.

The reality was that Damon had never been hers. Neither of them had ever committed to anything more than a brief, secretive fling, and that fling had been more than a year ago.

But they had a baby together. That meant something.

Surely Damon could have taken some time to re-assess. She took a deep breath and let it out slowly as she tried to rationalize the emotions that kept hitting her out of left field. Maybe she felt so shocked because, for the past year, even though she had left Damon, in a sense he had still been hers because, until Caroline, he had only dated sporadically.

Jemima had only lasted three weeks. Zara knew, be-cause she had checked.

As she sat down, her knee brushed the mouse pad of her laptop, jolting it. The screen saver dissolved and she found herself once more looking at the happy couple.

If Damon was getting married, that meant Caro-line would become Rosie's stepmother. Somehow that thought made her feel even more miserable.

If she was brutally honest, it was the knowledge that while Damon had been happy to sleep with her on the quiet, he clearly wanted marriage with the kind of woman who moved in his own social circle. Just seeing Caroline and Damon together ignited the same kind of deep, tender hurt Zara had experienced when she had left him and realized that, as formidably equipped as he was to find her, he had not cared enough to do so.

An unpleasant thought struck her. If Damon was planning on remarrying, it made all the sense in the world to clean out any skeletons in the cupboard. She and Rosie were a substantial skeleton.

Zara found herself back on her feet and pacing. Just seconds ago, she had felt chilled and more than a little sorry for herself. Now heat flamed through her, flushing her cheeks and making her heart pound.

It was no wonder Damon had left his sealed penthouse office and prowled the streets to find her. No wonder he was suddenly so keen to keep her close, even down to offering her a job and dangling a huge fee! Locked in his high-security office with all his ex-army cronies there to help him keep an eye on her—that was the definition of keeping her and Rosie, his two shady secrets, under wraps.

Zara tried to calm down. She had been feeling guilty about keeping Rosie a secret. She had even been feeling guilty about *who* she was, Petra's daughter, as if she had to apologize for her very existence.

But she wasn't the only one with secrets. She did not imagine that Caroline would be very happy to find out Damon had recently become a father.

Burning with indignation at Damon's double-dealing sneakiness and suddenly sick to death of living in the shadows and trying to be invisible—of feeling that she had committed some terrible crime just because she had slept with Damon a few times—she snatched up her phone. Unlocking it, she hit Redial on Damon's number. The second Damon picked up, Zara froze, caught in the kind of panicked state that usually had no part in her carefully organized life.

"Zara?" Damon's deep, curt voice sent adrenaline zinging through her veins.

Her throat seized up. A fraught second later, she disconnected the call.

Horrified that she'd lost control to the point that she had actually called Damon to find out whether he really was marrying Caroline—as if she had a right to ask that question—Zara placed the cell on the coffee table. She needed to pull herself together, to get back to the crisp, businesslike state of mind that had been her go-to with all things Damon over the past few weeks.

The phone chimed, almost stopping her heart. Damon's number glowed on the screen.

She stared at the cell as if it was a bomb about to explode, then kicked herself for not answering when a message popped up, informing her she had a new voice mail. With a sense of inevitability, she picked up the phone. Damon's message was edged with impatience. He wanted to know if Rosie was okay. He finished with the command that she call him.

When hell freezes over.

She should never have called him in the first place. With a jerky movement she did what she should have done just minutes ago—she turned the phone off altogether.

Still feeling crazily on edge, she looked in on Rosie, who had finally fallen into a deep sleep. Softly closing the door, Zara padded to the laundry and put on a load of clothes to wash, then did her last job of the night, which was preparing a bottle for Rosie's night feeding. As she tightened the screw lid on the bottle, the chime of her doorbell made her hand jerk.

Her first thought was that it was Damon, but she dismissed that possibility, because he was at the charity ball with the love of his life, Caroline. She glanced at the oven clock, disoriented to see that it was only nine thirty. It felt a whole lot later, probably because it had gotten dark so early.

Frowning, she put the bottle in the fridge and walked through the hall. Her front security light was on, illuminating the porch. Through the frosted glass side panels of the door she could make out a tall masculine figure, wearing a dark suit.

Adrenaline pumped. It *was* Damon.

Keeping the chain on, she opened the door a few inches.

Damon's gaze pinned hers. "You didn't call me back. What's wrong?"

The cool directness of his gaze paired with the

five o'clock shadow decorating his jaw gave Damon a remote edge that made her spine tighten. "Nothing's wrong." She tried for a neutral smile. "It was a mistake."

His cool gaze seemed to laser right through her. "Is it Rosie? I thought she might be sick."

"Rosie's fine. She's asleep." Despite knowing she shouldn't, but too furious not to, Zara took the chain off the hook and opened the door wide enough that she could look past Damon to where his car was parked. She wanted to know if Caroline was with him. Frustratingly, because the windows of his car were tinted, she couldn't see a thing. He could have half a dozen women in the car for all she knew.

A little impatiently, Damon's gaze recaptured hers. "Now that I'm here, we should talk. I think we need to get clear on a couple of things."

Such as his impending marriage to a woman who was perfect for him, and the fact that Zara and Rosie had the potential to ruin those plans.

Zara gave the sleek black car at her gate a last probing glare. "It's late. Can't we do this some other time?"

Damon gave her a look of disbelief. "It's only just past nine thirty."

Zara stared at Damon's jaw. Now that she was aware of the scary chinks in her armor when it came to him, she was determined to avoid eye contact where possible. The last thing she needed was for him to know how much he affected her. "I usually go to bed early, because I have to get up for Rosie in the night."

He leaned one shoulder against her porch wall and crossed his arms over her chest. "Okay, let's talk here."

"Can't we discuss whatever it is you want to talk about at work?"

"We could, but I thought you were concerned about keeping our relationship and Rosie under wraps."

Her gaze snapped to his, which was a problem because then she had trouble ripping it away. "We don't have a relationship."

His expression was infuriatingly calm. "But we do have a daughter."

And suddenly the gloves were off. "And I guess, at this point, keeping *our relationship* and Rosie under wraps suits you just fine, doesn't it?"

His brows jerked together. "Would you care to explain that?"

Bright light, intense enough to make her wince, washed across Zara's front lawn and lit up her porch. Her next-door neighbor's security lights had just come on. That meant that Edna Cross, who lived alone and seemed to be unusually inquisitive about every move Zara made, had no doubt logged that she had a visitor. Edna was the secretary of the local neighborhood watch group, and so was also likely now to be out with her flashlight and possibly even a digital camera. Any conversation on Zara's porch could no longer be considered private.

Damon stared in the direction of the high-powered light. His gaze narrowed. "There's someone standing on the other side of your hedge."

"My neighbor Edna Cross. She's head of the local neighborhood watch."

"That would explain the military-grade spotlights."

Ignoring the dryness of his voice and feeling embattled, Zara opened the door a little wider. She didn't want Damon in her house, but he clearly wasn't going to leave anytime soon and what she had to say needed to be said in private. "You had better come in."

With a last glance in the direction of Edna's silhouette, Damon stepped into Zara's hall, dwarfing it and making the space feel distinctly claustrophobic. Zara closed the door and, out of sheer habit, locked it, although the second she did so, it occurred to her that the one person she didn't want in her house was already inside.

As she turned, she realized Damon was waiting for her. She noticed that his tie was dragged loose, the top button of his white shirt was undone and his hair was disheveled as if he'd run his fingers through it repeatedly. All of it made him look even more sexily gorgeous. A pang of heat shot through her, making her clench her stomach. She could not believe she was turned-on, even in a marginal way when she was still so angry. Grimly, she reminded herself that it was far more likely that it was Caroline who had run her fingers through his hair.

Suddenly self-conscious about her leggings, the old sweater that dragged past her thighs and the fact that beneath all the soft layers she wasn't wearing a bra, Zara led the way to her sitting room.

Damon padded straight to the window that looked over Edna's property, pulled back the curtain and looked out. He lifted a hand. Seconds later, the glaring security lights flicked off. Amazing. Usually, if Edna felt impelled to investigate at night, the place was lit up like a landing strip for a good hour. In his blunt, masculine way, Damon had dealt with Edna by summarily checking her out and dismissing her.

He closed the curtains. "She's persistent."

Amusement invested his tone with an intimacy that spun Zara back to evenings spent together in his apartment watching movies and eating gourmet takeout. As he turned from the window, the easy humor was replaced by a flicker of masculine awareness that informed her that if she thought he hadn't noticed she wasn't wearing a bra, she was wrong.

Folding her arms across her chest, Zara indicated that Damon should have a seat. Unfortunately, he chose the seat she had been sitting in and her laptop was still sitting on the coffee table.

Panic gripped her. She couldn't remember whether she'd closed the video clip about Damon and Caroline, or not. In her rush to grab the laptop, all while avoiding getting too close to Damon, she brushed the mouse pad again and the screen saver dissolved.

Damon's gaze settled on the screen a split second before she snapped the laptop closed.

His expression answered the question. No, she had not closed down the video.

Cheeks burning, she found her briefcase, which was on a sideboard, and stowed the offending laptop away. When she turned, Damon was no longer seated, but prowling her small sitting room. He came to a stop in front of a small oil of a Medinian ancestor, one of the few family pieces left from her Atrides past. As he studied the gloomy picture, she felt a crazy sense of relief that, in keeping with her new identity and her new life, she had made it a rule not to have any family photos on show. Those were all kept in albums in a drawer in her room.

Plastering a bright smile on her face, she decided to grab the bull by the horns.

"I hear congratulations are in order."

Damon seemed to go very still. "What for, exactly?"

"Your engagement to Caroline Grant." Despite every effort at control, she couldn't quite keep the husky note from her voice. "No mystery now as to why you were so keen that I should come and work for you *and* bring Rosie along."

There was an odd moment of silence. "I'm guessing

that would be because you think I don't want Caro to find out that you've given birth to my child."

Caro. A red mist seemed to form in front of her eyes. Zara could feel her precarious hold on her temper slipping. "I don't think—I know. I can see why we never had a chance, quite apart from the fact that Caroline's *blonde.*"

Two steps and Damon had covered the distance between them. "As I recall, you were the one who laid down the ground rules for the time we spent together."

Zara flushed guiltily at the reminder that she'd had very good reasons for limiting their involvement. "Ground rules that suited you."

His brows jerked together. "Why, exactly, did they suit me?"

Zara met his gaze squarely. "Because I'm not your type."

"Which is…?"

"Blonde. Your wife was blonde. Caroline is blonde."

Damon pinched his nose, which made her even more furious, so she listed another three blonde socialites from the past. Even the names made her feel slightly crazy: Jenna, Hayley, *Tiffany.* They were all pretty, flirty names, nothing like Zara, which sounded somehow heftier. "It's all over the media that you like blondes. And not just blondes. You like a certain type of blonde. Basically, slim, elegant and rich. I'm not any of those—"

"Therefore, I couldn't possibly want you."

She drew a rapid breath and tried to calm down, but she couldn't seem to stop hemorrhaging the disappointment and anger she'd bottled up for over a year. At some point she must have taken a half step closer to Damon, close enough to feel the heat radiating off his body, smell the faint, enticing scents of soap and cologne.

She jabbed a finger at his chest. "Couldn't have said it better myself. Maybe if I had dyed my hair blonde or bought a wig, we would have had a chance at a real relationship." She delivered the kicker. "I don't even know why you slept with me in the first place."

His fingers closed around her upper arms. "That would be because I wanted you," he growled.

Shock reverberated through her at the statement. Both palms were flattened on his chest. She could feel the steady pound of his heart, feel the heat blasting off him. She could have pulled back, stepped free, because his hold was loose but, crazily, it was the last thing she wanted to do.

Something had happened to her in the last hour or so; it was as if all the emotions she had suppressed had burst free and, like a Pandora's box, she couldn't put them back in. And if that wasn't enough, being held close to Damon, having his complete, undivided attention even though they were arguing, filled her with an intoxicating elation.

She glared at him. "Wanted, as in past tense."

In answer, he fitted her close enough against him that she could feel his clear arousal. "Does this feel like past tense?"

She drew an impeded breath and tried to think, which was difficult when tingling heat was pouring through her and all she wanted to do was drown in the intense sensations. Damon bent his head and bit down gently on the sensitive lobe of one ear. A white-hot pang of heat lanced through her.

His jaw brushed her cheek, sending a sensual shiver through her. With a breathless effort, she resisted the urge to sag against him, even though her bones had turned to water. "You can't kiss me. You're engaged."

Irritation registered in Damon's gaze. "There's no engagement. As a matter of fact, Caroline and I are finished."

"Because of Rosie?"

"Rosie is part of it."

Damon lifted his head before she could ask if the rest of the reason was that he thought he now had some kind of responsibility toward them both. Afraid that she was pushing him away with her questioning, Zara's fingers gripped the lapels of his jacket, keeping him close. Minutes ago, she had been furious with Damon and determined to keep him at a distance but, in the space of a few seconds, somehow everything had changed. She took a deep breath, then finally asked the question that had tormented her ever since she had found Damon on her porch. "So...Caroline's not in your car?"

Damon gave her a look of disbelief. "Why would she be in my car?"

Relief and pleasure cascaded through Zara. He really wasn't going to marry Caroline, after all. The media had made up the story, and didn't Zara know how that went?

In some distant corner of her mind she knew she should be reacting differently; she shouldn't feel so happy and so relieved that Caroline was out of the picture.

Damon's expression was curiously intent. "What would you have done if Caroline had been in the car?"

Emotion surged through Zara. A list of scenarios flashed through her mind, all of which involved getting Caroline *out* of the car.

Damon grinned. "Thought so." He dropped his hands to her hips and pulled her closer still but, frustratingly, he didn't kiss her. Zara finally realized that he was waiting for her to make the next move.

Her mouth dry, her heart pounding—the memory of the kiss they'd shared that morning emboldening her—she lifted up on her toes, looped her arms around his neck and kissed him A split second later his arms came around her, locking her tight against him, as if he had missed her, as if he wanted her just as badly as she wanted him, as if he truly needed her close.

Ridiculous tears burned beneath her lids as she gave in to the simple pleasure of soaking up the heat and comfort of being back in Damon's arms. A comfort that she had tried to forget but which, against the odds, she still desperately needed.

He released his hold for the moment it took to shrug out of his jacket and toss it over the back of a chair. Another slow, drugging kiss, then she found herself slowly, irresistibly propelled backward into the narrow hall, which led to the bedrooms.

Damon lifted his head. In the deep shadows of the hall the narrow band of light that flowed out from the sitting room glanced across mouthwatering cheekbones and the rock-solid line of his jaw, turning his gray gaze molten. "This room?"

Dimly, Zara logged another opportunity to call a halt, to throw cold water on a passionate interlude she should already be regretting. Somehow, they had gone from zero to out-of-control passion in the space of minutes. The problem was, she had been so upset at the thought that Damon was engaged, then so relieved when he wasn't, that her rules for dealing with him had dissolved. She had become someone she barely recognized—fiercely possessive and determined to reclaim him, even if only for one night.

By pure luck Damon had chosen her room. She caught a glimpse of her bed with its rich red coverlet and pretty cushions, the deep blue drapes and the jewel-bright Medinian rug at the foot of her bed. The lush riot of color was very different from the restrained image she was so careful to project through the rest of the house, and in the way she dressed. She was suddenly unbearably conscious of her vulnerability in inviting Damon into a room that was an intimate and unashamed expression of herself.

But for the first time in years she didn't feel like apologizing for loving the flamboyant colors and rich fabrics of her childhood, for being Angel Atrides. With him, right now, she felt bold and passionate, and she knew exactly what she wanted.

"Yes."

Lifting up on her toes, she kissed Damon on the mouth, tangled her fingers with his and drew him into the room. Three steps and she felt the soft quilt of her bed brush the backs of her legs. Another kiss and she had managed to undo most of the buttons on Damon's shirt.

With an impatient movement, Damon completed the job and shrugged out of the shirt, revealing tanned and sleekly powerful shoulders, a broad chest and washboard abs.

She caught the quick gleam of his teeth. "Time this went."

His hands settled on her waist then swept upward, peeling her sweater and T-shirt up and over her head. The chill of the air was instantly replaced by the hot shock of skin-on-skin as he pulled her close.

Feeling a little vulnerable, because it had been more

than a year since they had made love, Zara buried her face in the curve of Damon's throat and allowed herself to be swamped by his masculine heat and scent. It occurred to her that being held in Damon's arms made her feel oddly like she had come home. She stiffened at the thought.

"What's wrong?"

With relief, she decided that the familiar timbre of Damon's voice provided the explanation for what she was really feeling. Not homecoming, but familiarity.

"Nothing. Absolutely nothing."

This time the hungry pressure of the kiss made her head swim.

Long seconds later, Damon cupped her breasts then bent and took one nipple into his mouth. Her breath came in as sensation coiled and burned for long aching moments then, with shocking abruptness, splintered.

Damon said something short and flat. A split second later she found herself lifted and deposited onto the bed. The cool softness of the quilt beneath her overheated skin was subtly shocking, but not as much as the disorienting fact that Damon had barely touched her and she had climaxed.

When he began peeling her leggings and panties down her legs, she automatically lifted her hips then felt hopelessly shy because her body wasn't as toned and sleek as it had been before she'd had Rosie. The chill of the air made her shiver, which was a convenient excuse to wriggle under the coverlet, dragging it high as Damon stripped off his pants.

When he straightened, she caught her breath at how beautiful he was with the murky half light turning his skin to bronze and making the trace of scars that criss-crossed his chest seem beautiful in a completely mas-culine way.

Damon retrieved something from his pants pocket, a condom. She watched as he sheathed himself and the blunt awareness of what they were about to do hit home. Somehow, in the space of one day, they had gone from cool, businesslike distance to passionate lovemaking. The knowledge should have made her feel disoriented and angsty, instead, for the first time in a year, she felt oddly settled and, for want of a better word, happy.

She wasn't yet ready to examine exactly what it was she still felt for Damon. For now, all she wanted was to forget the heartache and loneliness of the past year and simply *feel*. For this one night it was enough that Damon was hers.

Damon joined her in the bed, flipping the cover-let aside as he did so. Zara surreptitiously attempted to drag the sheet over her breasts, but he stymied her plan by pulling her close so that she was half-sprawled against his chest.

Pleasure cascaded through her at the blazing heat of his body, the clean, faintly musky scent of his skin and the automatic, sensual way they fitted together, almost as if more than a year hadn't passed since they had last made love.

"Don't cover yourself," he said quietly. "You're beautiful."

She cupped his jaw, enjoying the faintly abrasive feel of his five o'clock shadow. "It's been a while."

He stopped in the process of trailing his fingers from the small of her back to the curve of her bottom. "No one else?"

She tried to muster up some indignation, but with the slow, enticing stroke of his hands it was hard to concentrate. "Why would there be anyone else? I was pregnant, then having a baby. There was barely time to breathe."

An entirely masculine brand of satisfaction registered in his gaze. "My baby."

He rolled, taking her beneath him. The fiery, seductive heat of Damon's weight pressing her down into the bed made it incredibly difficult to marshal her thoughts. And why would she want to think?

As much as she might deny it, this was what she had missed so much and still craved. The plain fact was that she had never gotten over the attraction that had hit her the very first time she had walked into his office. It was the reason she had slept with Damon in the first place, the reason she had let him back into her life. It was probably also the reason why there had been no other man in her life.

Zara went still inside as a thought she had resolutely suppressed over the last year once again surfaced.

Could she be in love with Damon?

She desperately dismissed the sudden tension that gripped her, because loving Damon was a worst-case scenario...*unless he fell in love with her.*

Suddenly, intensely curious about how he felt, she cupped his face. "Would it have mattered if there was someone else?"

"You were pregnant with my child."

The answer was flat and unequivocal, and sent a sharp thrill through her. Despite being a modern woman, she couldn't help but adore that Damon was possessive of her, even if it was only because she had borne his child. And his response was proof that he felt something genuine, even if only sexual desire.

Although, in her heart of hearts, she didn't want just the desire, she thought fiercely.

She was very much afraid that she *was* falling for Damon, despite all the reasons they should never be in the same room together, let alone in the same bed.

But perhaps making love could create a bond that would hold. And maybe, just maybe, that bond would be strong enough to survive the revelation of her past.

Dipping his head, Damon kissed her. Feeling suddenly acutely vulnerable, Zara gripped his shoulders, arching against the blunt pressure of penetration as he slowly, carefully entered her. When they were fully joined, Damon stopped, his darkened gaze locking with hers.

"Are you sure this is all right? It's not so long since the birth."

With the aching heat of him deep inside her, it was difficult to think. "It's been four months." And before that, nine months. In total it had been thirteen long months since they had last made love. She inhaled at the sensations that gripped her, some familiar, some even more intense than she remembered.

"I'll take it easy."

In answer, she pressed closer still. An agonizing second later, Damon began to move. The heated, stirring pleasure that, lately, had only been a part of her dreams, wound tight, pressing all the air from her lungs until it finally peaked, splintering into the night.

Seven

Damon stirred, awakened by the heavy drumming of rain on the roof and the first stirrings of arousal as Zara trailed her hand down his abdomen. The silky curtain of her hair brushed across his chest as she bent and kissed him slowly and deliberately on the mouth. Her hand slid lower, found him and gently squeezed.

He held on to his control, just. "The last time this happened, I seem to remember we got pregnant."

She waved the foil packet of a condom at him.

"Resourceful."

Long minutes later, Zara collapsed on his chest and he rolled, taking her with him so that they lay sprawled together. The rain had stopped and the wind had dropped, making the night seem almost unnaturally still and quiet.

After long minutes, she readjusted her position, so that her head was snuggled into the curve of his shoulder and neck. One hand trailed over his jaw.

"Do you know why we made love?" she murmured sleepily.

Damon stiffened at the question. "Why?"

Zara yawned. "Can't resist you. It's fate, kismet. Last thing either of us need."

There was a curious, vibrating silence following the slightly slurred pronouncement. But the tension, Damon realized after a few seconds, was his and his alone. Zara didn't require an answer because she had fallen asleep.

She couldn't resist him.

Unbidden, warmth and forbidden delight unfolded in Damon. That was a first, he thought ruefully. But then there had never been anything calculated or pragmatic about making love with Zara. It had always been spontaneous. This time they had actually made it to a bed.

He didn't know about either fate or kismet. He preferred to operate with cool, hard facts. If Zara couldn't resist him, then that dovetailed nicely with his plans for the future…and the undeniable fact that he was having a whole lot of trouble resisting her too.

The next time Damon awoke it was to a small, unfamiliar sound.

Rosie was awake.

He noted the time on the digital clock on the bedside table: three thirty. If he didn't miss his guess, because Rosie was so young, she needed feeding in the night. Carefully disentangling himself from Zara, he found his pants and quickly pulled them on. As he did so, he found himself automatically mulling over Zara's declaration that she couldn't resist him.

Fierce satisfaction filled him at that fact, even though desire itself was uncomfortably akin to the kind of dangerous, unstable emotions he was careful to avoid. If they were going to continue—and now that he had gotten Zara back in his bed, he fully intended they would— he needed to find a way to control the relationship.

Grimly, he noted that the hot, out-of-control sex could have been because he hadn't made love in a year, ever since Zara had left his bed. That fact, in itself, was disturbing.

He had dated a number of beautiful, interesting women. Caroline was a case in point. Any man with red blood cells in his veins would have wanted her, and yet he had not even been vaguely interested in taking her to bed.

Because he had not been able to stop thinking about Zara.

And there was his problem, the same kind of obsessive behavior that had dogged his father, his uncle Tyler and now Ben. The kind of behavior Damon had sworn off all of his adult life and which experience had taught him he could not afford.

Not bothering with a shirt, he stepped out into the hall. It wasn't difficult to find where Rosie slept, since there was only one other bedroom in the cottage.

When he opened the door, it squeaked. Cursing beneath his breath, he checked on Zara, who still seemed to be sleeping deeply, before going to Rosie. The baby waved her arms at him so he picked her up and propped her on one bare shoulder, figuring that was the easiest and most stable way to hold her if he was going to attempt to feed her.

Grabbing a small shawl that was folded over the end of her cot, he draped that across her back in case she got cold, and made his way to the small kitchen. He closed the door, which also squeaked, before switching on the light. Absently, he noted that was two doors that needed oil on their hinges.

He immediately saw that the baby bag sat on the bench. Although he figured that Zara probably had a bottle already prepared in the fridge since she must do regular night feeds.

He opened the door and saw it straight off. Guessing it needed to be warmed, he ran the bottle under hot water for a minute or two. When it was done, he checked the temperature of the milk. He seemed to remember, after visiting friends who had a baby, that the milk needed to be lukewarm, so he tested it by shaking a little onto the back of his hand.

"Seems good to go."

Rosie, who had half twisted around on his shoulder

to check what he was doing, made a cooing sound, patted him on the jaw and smiled, flashing the clean edge of one pearly tooth.

Damon was momentarily transfixed by the sight of his daughter's first tooth, his chest swelling with a raw hit of emotion. If he had planned on being distant and disconnected from his daughter, that idea had just crashed and burned.

Opening the kitchen door just enough to allow a sliver of light to flow into the sitting room, he sat in an armchair and attempted to resettle Rosie in the crook of his arm, all while juggling the bottle. But if he had thought Rosie would allow herself to be carefully repositioned while there was a full bottle of milk tantalizingly within reach, he was wrong. She wriggled and squirmed, her gaze zeroing in on the bottle. The instant it got close enough, strong small hands wrapped around the neck and almost wrenched the formula from his grasp.

She drained the milk in sixty seconds flat, spat out the nipple, then with imperiousness attempted to fling the empty bottle away. Damon found himself grinning as he fielded the bottle, placed it on the coffee table and rose to his feet with his daughter in his arms. When he had noticed Rosie's eyes the previous day, he had seen himself, but right now she was *definitely* her mother's daughter.

In that moment he understood how people became so centered on their children that they married when they'd sworn off marriage, and made career U-turns that were detrimental to success. The answer was simple: their priorities changed because they were besotted by the baby.

Rosie's face screwed up, her pale skin flushing. For a heart-stopping moment he thought she was going to cry. He seemed to remember that after Rosie had been fed the previous day, Zara had put her over her shoulder to burp her, so he figured he should do that next.

After circling the small room a couple of times and carefully rubbing her small back, Rosie made a hiccuping sound and spit up on his shoulder. Feeling ridiculously proud that Rosie had burped right on cue, he headed back to the kitchen, found a paper towel and cleaned around her mouth, before blotting the milk from his shoulder.

After disposing of the paper towel in the trash can he found beneath the counter, he carried his daughter back to the sitting room.

"So, what do we do now?"

Rosie patted his jaw again, as if she was fascinated by the roughness of his five o'clock shadow and, at that point, Damon noted a certain sogginess at her rear end.

"Problem solved. We change your diaper."

Rosie made a small crowing sound, as if that was a hilarious idea, so he returned to the kitchen and did a brief search through the baby bag, finding disposable diapers and baby wipes. Walking through to the sitting room, he carefully laid Rosie down on the carpet. Five minutes later, he had the dirty diaper off and the clean diaper fitted. Feeling a sense of achievement, he bagged up the dirty diaper and soiled wipes and placed them in the trash. After washing his hands, he collected a now-sleepy Rosie and carried her back to her room and tucked her into her crib.

After watching her for long minutes to make sure she really had fallen asleep, he walked back to the bedroom. It was four thirty; an hour had passed while he'd fed and changed Rosie. In that time, Zara hadn't moved and still seemed soundly asleep. With effort, he curbed the instinct to get back into bed with her. If he did that, he wouldn't be able to resist making love to her again, which would be counterproductive, given that his first priority had to be control.

Collecting his shirt and shoes, he walked back to the sitting room and finished dressing. He shrugged into his jacket and checked that he had his cell before he let himself out of the house. As he walked down the steps, the next-door neighbor's obnoxiously bright security lights came on.

Damon frowned. If Zara and Rosie were going to stay in the cottage, he would ensure that the motion sensors for those security lights were repositioned so they would no longer be triggered by movement on Zara's property. But, now that he knew Zara was the mother of his child, *now that Zara was back in his bed*, he did not intend for her and Rosie to remain in a suburban cottage with minimal security.

The solution he had arrived at the previous day settled in more firmly.

It was logical, practical and would cut through a whole lot of red tape. It also had the added advantage of nixing dangerously unstable emotions and dampening any media hype.

A marriage of convenience.

Zara's alarm pulled her out of sleep at six thirty.

She groped for the clock. The low buzz ceased and she stared at the numbers that glowed in the pitch dark of early dawn, amazed at the time. By some miracle, Rosie had slept through the night.

Bracing herself, she switched on the bedside lamp. Gold light flooded her room, making her blink and pushing home the reality that she was alone in the bed. Although she had known Damon was gone the second she had reached across the cold expanse of the bed to get to the alarm.

Heated memories cascaded through her, making her blush. Jackknifing, she sat up. Cold air raised gooseflesh on her skin. Shivering, she dragged the quilt up around her chin, because, of course, she was naked, having spent the night making love to Damon. Claiming him physically.

Another memory took center stage. In the moments before she had fallen asleep, she had blurted out something about not being able to resist Damon.

Another wave of embarrassed heat burned through

her. She could vaguely remember the silence after she had made her pronouncement, the stiffening of his shoulder beneath her head—probably because he didn't find her irresistible—then nothing more because she had dropped into a deep, dreamless sleep.

Feeling mortified at the way she had exposed a very private weakness, she pushed the thick feather duvet aside and scrambled out of bed. The icy chill of the marble-smooth, polished wood floor struck through her bare feet as she toed on her slippers and quickly wrapped herself in the thick fluffy robe that was hooked on the back of her door.

She shouldn't feel embarrassed, she thought a little desperately. But it was hard to blot out the fact that Damon hadn't responded to her declaration.

Opening her bedroom door, she glanced down the hall and through the sitting room to the kitchen. She tensed when she realized she was looking for Damon on the off chance he was sitting on the couch doing business on his phone or in the kitchen making breakfast.

Of course, Damon wasn't here. His side of the bed had been stone cold; he had been gone for hours. Her mood plummeted even further. He had probably left at a run not long after she had gone to sleep.

She opened Rosie's door. Rosie was still fast asleep. Gently, so as not to wake her, she checked her diaper, which seemed inordinately dry. Frowning, Zara walked through to the kitchen and saw the night feed bottle, which had been rinsed and was sitting on the kitchen counter. A quick check of the trash can confirmed there was also a diaper wrapped in a plastic bag sitting on top.

Clearly, Damon had not left as quickly as she had thought. She closed the cupboard door. The last thing she would have expected was for Damon to feed and change Rosie, but that was exactly what had happened.

Moving on automatic, she put hot water on to boil for tea. She made herself a piece of toast, smeared it with butter and the fig-and-ginger jam she'd made with fruit from the fig tree in the backyard, then prepared a morning feeding for Rosie.

She took a half-hearted bite of the toast, barely tasting it. She guessed she should be happy that Damon was interested in forming a relationship with Rosie, since it was less than a day since he had found out he was a father. But she couldn't help thinking that Damon's interest in her, Zara, was depressingly linked with his focus on his daughter and that any idea that she and Damon could remain lovers was majorly flawed.

First, Damon had shown up at her house not for her, but because he had thought Rosie was ill. Second, yes, he had made love to Zara, but that had probably happened because she had literally thrown herself at him.

Another even more horrifying thought froze her in place. Damon was probably under the impression that since she'd had his baby, and now had managed to get him back into her bed, that she was angling for marriage.

She groaned inwardly and ate some more toast. It was no wonder he had left in the night without waking

her. He had come for Rosie's sake and Zara had not only
seduced him, but made the silly mistake of revealing
how much she wanted him.

Given that Damon had never once said he wanted
to be in a committed relationship with her, even when
they were first sleeping together, the odds that he did
now were bleak. Damon's true motivation in showing
up at her house was his caring for Rosie.

Wiping crumbs from her fingers, she carried her
plate to the sink and washed and dried it. As she was
putting the plate away a brief flash of the kiss they'd
shared in her office stopped her in her tracks. She did
not know if Damon had known about Rosie at that point,
but she had been clear on the fact that he had wanted
her.

Closing the cupboard door, she straightened. It was
also a fact that Damon had walked back into her life
weeks *before* he had known about Rosie. And he hadn't
just walked back in, he had pushed his way back into
her life, insistently forging a business link and employing people she knew for a fact he did not need. That
all pointed to the fact that Damon's desire for her was
genuine and persistent.

Feeling suddenly cheered, she wrapped chilled fingers around her gently steaming mug of tea and sipped.
There was hope. She just had to hold her nerve and look
for the right opportunity to tell him who she was, in
such a way that he wouldn't despise her.

Feeling buoyed, she checked on Rosie, who was

still sleeping soundly. Zara quickly showered, dried off and wrapped herself in the robe while she searched out something to wear.

Dressing wasn't normally a problem, but today she felt the feminine need to dress for attractiveness as well as for business. Unfortunately, most of her suits were quite plain and, owing to the fact that she had lost a little weight, were becoming a little loose and shapeless.

Happy that her figure had improved, but annoyed at the wardrobe dilemma, she flicked through the closet. Her fingers lingered on an outfit she had worn before she had gotten pregnant.

She pulled out the blue dress and the fitted black jacket that went with it. It was a deceptively simple but gorgeous outfit she hadn't been able to fit into since her pregnancy.

The dress was also soft and warm and extremely comfortable, but would it fit? She held the blue dress against her and stared into the full-length mirror, which was hung on the inside of her closet door. The sapphire blue did great things for her skin, giving it a honey glow and making her eyes look brighter and her hair more lustrous. The dress also had a V neckline, which showed the merest shadow of cleavage, but wasn't too blatant.

After slipping into clean underwear, she pulled on the dress, which—happily—was made of a stretchy, bouclé material. Her figure was still more rounded than it had once been, and her waist wasn't as narrow, but the dress was unexpectedly forgiving. To her surprise the jacket also fitted, cinching in neatly at her waist.

She studied her reflection, her breath momentarily suspended. With her hair still knotted on top of her head from her shower, and dark tendrils clinging to her neck, she looked businesslike, but subtly, classily sexy.

With quick movements, she brushed out her hair and coiled it up into a loose knot, then applied smoky makeup to her eyes and a layer of pink gloss to her mouth.

She had just fitted blue-and-silver earrings to her lobes when Rosie woke up and began crowing happily to herself. Checking her watch and groaning because she was fast running out of time if she wanted to leave early, Zara hurried into Rosie's room.

Rosie stopped crying the instant she spotted her mother, held out her small arms and smiled her wide, gummy smile, which now contained one tiny, gleaming half tooth.

Warmth and a fierce, tender love suffused Zara as she lifted her daughter out of her crib and cuddled her close. Rosie's soft, sweet baby scent rose to Zara's nostrils and the anxious fears around being in a relationship with Damon, if that was even possible, drifted away.

In moments like these, *everything* was worth it— the months of worry and uncertainty, the solitary birth without anyone to support her except her midwife. The effort and frustration of learning all the things a mother needed to know without her own mother to show her.

Half an hour later, after feeding and changing Rosie and dressing her in a cute pink playsuit, Zara finally got Rosie back to sleep in her fleece-lined car seat. She draped a warm fluffy blanket around her daughter and settled a cute pink beanie on her head so she would stay cozily asleep. Then Zara carried the car seat out to the hall.

After propping Rosie's portable crib beside the car seat, Zara rinsed out the used bottle and put it into the dishwasher. She checked her watch. Shock reverberated through her when she saw that it was eight o'clock. If she wanted to avoid Damon's driver and keep her independence, she needed to leave, *now*.

Moving quickly, she found a pair of black boots that would go perfectly with the dress and slipped them on. She zipped the baby bag closed and set it in the hallway, then found her handbag and cell. As she looped the strap of her handbag over one shoulder, the sound of a car made her stiffen. She peered through the narrow glass panes of her front door just in time to see a gleaming black car glide to a halt outside her front gate.

Her heart thumped once, hard. She was too late; Damon had second-guessed her and sent the car early.

Eight

Feeling distinctly outmaneuvered, Zara tried to check out the driver, but the windows of the car were too darkly tinted.

Another pump of adrenaline made her stomach churn as she noted the kind of car Damon had sent. She had hoped for a taxi, and had been resigned to a company car, but the glossy curves of a long, low sports car did not bode well. It looked like the car Damon had been driving last night. A split second later, Damon climbed out from behind the wheel.

Feeling suddenly vulnerable, she opened the door a split second before Damon could knock and tried not to notice how broodingly masculine he looked in a dark suit teamed with a black V-neck T-shirt. A pair of dark glasses added a remote edge that seemed to negate the intimate things they had done in bed just hours ago.

Movement off to the right caught her eye. Her heart sank when she saw Edna, who, if Zara wasn't mistaken, was in the process of noting Damon's license plate and the make and model of his car.

"I thought you were sending a driver."

"I'm the driver." Damon's glittering gaze swept over her, making her feel acutely conscious of how sexy the blue dress was and the fact that, from his height, he could probably see more than just the hint of cleavage she had noted in the mirror. "I thought we should spend some time together before we go into the office."

Desperate to control the sudden warmth in her cheeks, Zara switched her attention back to Edna, who was now taking down details about Damon himself. No doubt height, weight, hair color and any other distinguishing features.

Although she wouldn't find any of those unless she managed to get Damon naked.

"What do you mean, 'spend some time together'?"

"There's a little café along the waterfront. It's quiet. The coffee's good, and we could walk on the beach, if you want."

In public? A small shudder went through her at the thought that they could get snapped together by a reporter. If that happened, her quiet life of anonymity, and the chance she needed to tell Damon who she was before the media spoiled everything, would be gone. "I don't think that's a good idea."

"We need to talk about Rosie and I'd prefer a more private setting than the office."

Zara noticed a bright blue hatchback driving slowly down the street, as if the driver was searching for an address. The hatchback glided past. Maybe she was being paranoid, but after what had happened yesterday, she could not help the crawling suspicion that the driver was a reporter, in which case, the sooner they left the better.

"A walk on the beach is not a good idea right now," she said hurriedly. "Rosie's sleeping." And if that had been a reporter, they could be followed to the beach. "We should go straight to the office."

Damon lifted a brow. "The sooner you start working, the sooner you can finish up and leave?"

Zara picked up the baby bag and portable crib and handed them to Damon, before collecting Rosie, who was still sound asleep in the car seat. Zara set the car seat down on the step and locked the front door. By the time she'd returned the key to her bag, Damon was back and had picked up the car seat.

Zara hurried after Damon, stepped outside her front gate and stopped dead. Last night when she had seen Damon's car, it had been dark, but now, in the full light of day she realized Damon was driving the same car he'd had when they had been dating.

The very last time they had made love, before she

had disappeared, had been in *that* car. Memories she had ruthlessly suppressed unfolded. Her acute emotionalism at being pregnant with Damon's child coupled with her need to be with him just one last time, to store up memories. The awful feeling of emptiness when she had thought she would never see him again.

The car flashed and beeped as Damon unlocked it. "What's wrong?"

Zara quickly smoothed out her expression. Note to self, she thought grimly, if she wanted to conceal her emotions, she needed to get a pair of dark glasses herself.

"Nothing," she said brightly.

She slipped into the front passenger seat while Damon strapped Rosie into the rear. As Damon slid behind the wheel of the Audi, Zara fastened her seat belt, then turned to check on the baby. She noticed a second safety seat, which Damon had installed in the back. A much nicer, more expensive seat than the basic model she had bought.

Suddenly, any notion that Rosie could be just a novelty for Damon evaporated. He must have gone shopping for the seat the previous afternoon. If he had gone to the trouble of buying a car seat, then that meant he was serious about fatherhood.

As Damon pulled away from the curb, Zara sank back into the luxurious seat. "I don't mind accepting a lift today, but in the future, I would prefer to take my own car to work."

Damon braked for a traffic light before accelerating through an intersection and joining the flow of cars heading for the central city. "If you want to drive your car to work, you can have Ben's parking space."

She glared at Damon. "You could have let me use that today!"

His gaze, still frustratingly masked by the dark glasses, connected with hers. "I didn't want to risk you not turning up for work."

"I agreed to work for you. I honor my agreements."

Damon stopped for another light, this one in the busy hub of downtown. "You walked out on me a year ago."

She dragged her gaze from the taut cut of Damon's cheekbones, the clean line of his jaw. Her heart was pounding again, but this time for an entirely different reason. It suddenly occurred to her that no employer manipulated and then personally drove an employee to work because they couldn't risk them not showing up. Certainly not a billionaire like Damon.

And he had refused to accept just any assistant; Damon had wanted *her*. He wanted her in his bed *and* at his work.

She was abruptly certain that whatever Damon was feeling, it wasn't just sexual attraction.

Her mood soared. Suddenly, Damon wanting her *as a person*, maybe even falling for her, seemed...possible.

Minutes later, using a key card to gain entrance, dim shadow swamped the car as Damon took the ramp down into the underground garage of his building. Zara's stomach did a nervous flip at the sheer familiarity of the garage as Damon removed his sunglasses, killed the engine and exited the Audi.

Before he could walk around the front of the car and help her out, Zara hurriedly unfastened her seat belt, collected her handbag and swung the door of the sleek, low car wide.

As she exited the car and straightened, she found herself close enough to Damon that when she inhaled she caught the clean scent of his skin, the utterly familiar tang of his cologne. In the dimness of the garage the impact of his gaze made her breath catch in her throat. Yesterday she would have kept her manner neutral and breezed past him, but today was a new world.

Hooking the strap of her bag over her shoulder, she allowed Damon to close the door with a *thunk*. Before she could lose her nerve, she met his gaze. "Thanks for being so understanding about Rosie. The last thing I wanted was for you to feel trapped into fatherhood." And trapped into a relationship with her.

Balancing herself by resting one palm on his shoulder, she lifted up on her toes to kiss him on the cheek.

Damon cupped her neck, stopping her from stepping back. The heat of his palm burned into her skin as, slowly and deliberately, he bent his head and kissed her on the mouth.

Long seconds later, her legs feeling as limp as noodles, she stumbled back a half step. It occurred to her that while the garage was a secure one, it did still service a number of clients.

"Maybe we shouldn't kiss in public," she said a little breathlessly. As soon as she said the words she realized that Damon would pick up on the clear implication that he could continue to kiss her in private.

Surprise and a glint of masculine satisfaction registered in his gaze as he caught her close and kissed her again. The kind of kiss shared by couples who were not just lovers, but who were in a real relationship. Couples who liked one another. The very nature of it filled Zara with hope because she was certain that in the past few minutes they had turned some kind of corner.

As he released her, Zara noticed a blue-suited janitor and froze. As quiet as their conversation had been, in the cavernous garage it had echoed. From his frozen posture, the janitor had heard every word.

Zara's breath froze in her throat as he disappeared from sight behind a large concrete pillar. For a split second she tried to buy into the fantasy that maybe the janitor hadn't heard. And if he had, who would he tell, anyway?

Potentially everyone.

Now thoroughly rattled, the warm sense of togetherness with Damon splintered, Zara freed Rosie from her car seat and lifted her out. As she straightened, in her hurry, the back of her head caught the frame of the Audi's door, which was lower than that of her own car. She winced and straightened. As she did so, her bag, which she'd hooked over her shoulder, flopped to the ground, sending items scattering.

Damon steadied her. "Babe, are you all right?"

Muttering that she was fine, Zara clutched Rosie's warm, soft little body securely against her own and rubbed at the sore patch.

Babe. The surprise of the endearment was so distracting that Zara forgot she'd dropped her handbag and stepped back. Something crunched beneath her heel.

Her mood plummeted even further. That would be her phone. A little awkwardly, she retrieved it. A cracked screen, and the insides were undoubtedly mashed too. It would be a miracle if it ever worked again.

Before she could pick up any other items, Damon collected the keys and compact that had scattered, dropped them into her bag and handed the bag to her. Seconds later, he collected Rosie's things, locked the car and indicated the elevator. "If you're worried about the phone, don't be. I was giving you a company phone in any case."

Zara walked into the familiar private elevator. As Damon joined her, the feeling of disorientation that she was actually returning to work for Damon intensified.

The first person Zara saw as she stepped into the foyer was Howard Prosser, Damon's office manager. Howard's look of surprise that Zara was holding a baby informed her that Damon had been true to his word. If he hadn't confided the fact that Rosie was his child to Howard, then he hadn't told anyone.

Zara adjusted her grip on Rosie, who was becoming restless, and tried to look as if her relationship with Damon was as casual and incidental as Howard clearly thought it to be.

Damon glanced at a file Howard handed him. "Zara's just filling in for a few days, until the McCall takeover is complete."

Howard looked distinctly grumpy. "That's not likely to happen unless you track down whoever has that block of missing voting shares."

Damon's palm briefly cupped her elbow as he urged her toward the door to her old office. The small, proprietorial touch sent a small thrill of awareness through her.

"A rival firm's been buying shares," he explained as he set the baby bag and portable crib down behind the desk. "That wouldn't be a problem except that ten percent of the voting shares are held by an anonymous shareholder, something that should never have happened. The net result is we've been having difficulty securing a majority of the stock."

Zara set her handbag down beside the desk. "Why shouldn't the shares be held by an anonymous shareholder? Surely that happens all the time."

"Not with voting shares. And these were Tyler's personal shares. By rights they should have remained in the family, since they guaranteed the majority vote. At some point, and for some reason I can't fathom, he must have sold them. We'd buy them back but, unfortunately, there's no record of the transaction."

Zara shifted Rosie from one arm to another and became immediately aware that the baby needed a diaper change. As she rummaged in the baby bag for a changing pad and a diaper, Rosie wriggled and craned around and sent Damon a smile that was literally blinding. She held out her arms as if she had already recognized that Damon was her daddy.

Damon lifted a brow. "May I?"

"She needs a diaper change."

"If that's supposed to frighten me, you're failing."

"Because you're already an old hand at it, having changed her diaper last night."

Damon's gaze caught hers. "I figured you could use the sleep."

Zara's cheeks burned as she considered exactly why she had needed the sleep and, with an odd reluctance, because up until now Rosie had been solely hers, she allowed Damon to take his daughter. As he balanced Rosie against one broad shoulder, his hand cradling her head, Zara experienced a curious sinking feeling in the pit of her stomach. She should look away, she thought a little desperately, except that she couldn't. There was something about Damon cradling Rosie that was utterly mesmerizing.

With effort, she dragged her gaze from the too-fascinating juxtaposition of Rosie's cute pink beanie and the tough line of Damon's jaw and concentrated on laying the changing pad out on the desk. While Damon was dealing with the dirty diaper, she found baby wipes, ointment and a plastic bag.

When Rosie was freshly changed, Damon picked her up as if she was a fragile piece of porcelain, hugged her close for a few seconds, then handed her back to Zara. "By the way, I've received confirmation that Ben and Emily are on Medinos, staying at a house we own there. I've arranged to fly out in the company jet and talk to Ben."

Sudden crashing disappointment hit Zara. A trip to Medinos and back meant Damon would be away for the best part of four days. When she didn't know how much time they had before the media discovered Damon had a daughter, four days was an eternity.

"Can't you just talk to Ben on the phone?"

"He would have to answer his phone for that to happen." Damon walked to the windows and stared out at the view as if he was mulling something over. When he turned, the morning light threw his face into shadow. "Since it'll be a working trip," he said quietly, "I want you and Rosie to come with me."

As shocking as the idea of flying overseas anywhere with Damon was, the idea of going to Medinos irresistibly appealed. For one thing, because she'd been absent for so long it wasn't likely that she'd be recognized. And the trip could prove a lifeline because it would buy her more time with Damon away from the Auckland reporters. It would also allow her to check out her mother's safe-deposit box. Added to that, traveling in the Magnum company jet would cost her nothing.

A cautious sense of relief gripped her. Could it be, after so much had gone wrong with her life, that her luck had finally turned? "Okay."

Damon didn't try to hide his disbelief. "You agree?"

"Either way I'll still be working, and at least it'll stop that nosy reporter from sniffing around." Zara struggled to keep her expression bland when what she really wanted to do was give in to the relief and either grin or cry. She checked her watch and saw it was time for Rosie's feeding. She grabbed at the excuse to do something, anything, that would distract her from revealing to Damon just how important it was for her to get to Medinos.

Frowning, Damon perched on one corner of the desk as she made a production of finding the insulated container that held Rosie's bottle.

"There's just one glitch—we'll need to get Rosie a passport. Walter can probably pull some strings and get one in a day or—"

"Rosie already has a passport." Zara could feel her cheeks burning as she directed what she hoped was a matter-of-fact smile in Damon's direction. As if it wasn't at all unusual for a four-month-old baby to have a passport. As if they hadn't been planning to go to Medinos all along. "When do we leave?"

There was a small silence during which the sounds

of the office registered: a phone ringing, the low burr of Howard's voice, the tapping of a keyboard.

Damon checked his watch, his expression oddly grim. "The only holdup would have been getting Rosie a passport. Since you've taken care of that already, I'll call the flight crew. We leave this afternoon."

Nine

An hour later Damon gave up on his efforts to call Ben, who had clearly turned his phone off, or more probably thrown it into the deep blue Mediterranean Sea.

He paced to the enormous glass doors that stretched the length of one entire wall in his office. The heavy cloud from last night had gone and the day was clear and dry, the sun sparkling on the harbor and gleaming off the glossy, expensive yachts tied up in the viaduct. But the view, spectacular as it was, barely impinged on his thoughts. At this point, even Ben was the least of his problems.

Zara had gotten Rosie a passport.

There was no point doing that unless Zara had intended to leave the country with Rosie. Disappearing from sight again as she had tried to do just over a year ago.

Broodingly, he considered that maybe Zara had only wanted to take a vacation? The problem with that scenario was that he knew Zara didn't have that kind of money. Walter had made a few discreet inquiries, so Damon knew that in financial terms, Zara was struggling to keep her head above water. The fact was, *he* had been propping up her finances for months, by hiring people he didn't need.

If Zara couldn't afford a holiday there was only one scenario left, she had been planning on leaving the country with Rosie and, in the process, *leaving him*.

But why start a new business if she was planning on emigrating? None of it made sense.

With sudden decision, he walked through to Walter's office. "I need you to run a security check on Zara."

Walter looked up from a thick legal pad on which he was making notes. "Didn't we do that last year?"

"Not in depth." Since Zara was fresh out of college, he had just asked for a standard check, which was relatively superficial, establishing whether or not there were any criminal convictions or debt issues that might compromise business loyalties, checking that qualifications and references were authentic. Since Zara had just graduated with an honors degree, and had been referred by a business acquaintance, an in-depth check had seemed like overkill.

"What exactly are you worried about?" Walter's gaze narrowed. "The baby's not yours."

"Rosie's mine."

Walter gave him a bland look. "Knew it as soon as I saw her."

Despite his irritation, Damon had to stop himself from grinning. "That obvious?"

"'Fraid so." Walter shook his head. "At least the baby explains why Zara left. Although it still doesn't really add up."

Damon's brows jerked together. "Explain."

"Disclosure. It's big with women."

Damon waited for more; when it didn't come he kept a grip on his irritation. "Walter, you're going to have to use more words."

Walter sat back in his chair. "Margot made me join this group for men who have difficulty communicating—"

"I thought Margot liked the strong, silent type."

Walter gave him a stony look. "Do you want to hear this or not? According to the group facilitator, women actually like to talk about their emotional lives. It's called disclosure. Darned irritating and a waste of time if you ask me, but Margot has got some bee in her bonnet because, *apparently*, I don't discl—"

"Let's take it back to Zara."

Walter blinked as if he'd just returned from a dark place. "Okay. Simple equation. Zara was in love with you, so, being a woman, she should have told you about the pregnancy."

Damon's chest locked up. He felt like he'd just been kicked by a mule. "What makes you think Zara was in love with me?"

Walter gave him an "are you serious?" look. "Zara has all the raw materials of a sergeant major or a general. She could organize a war. So, it figures, why else would she let down her guard and sleep with you if she wasn't, you know, *in love*?"

Damon's jaw tightened on a complex surge of emotions—heat, raw possessiveness, unaccountable relief. An hour ago, any idea that Zara was in love with him would have had him warily backing off. But that was before she had calmly admitted that she already had a passport for Rosie. The passport was a game changer because it signaled that Zara and Rosie were leaving, and he did not want that to happen.

"So why do you think, if Zara was in love with me, that she didn't 'disclose' the pregnancy?"

Walter looked reflective. "Zara's a decisive woman. Maybe she just got tired of you." He nodded his head. "Yep, that's a pretty clear-cut reason for leaving."

Damon restrained his irritation with difficulty. He could see why Margot had sent Walter to counseling. "She didn't get tired of me."

Walter drummed his fingers on the desk. "I guess, since she's back."

Damon's jaw tightened. *And* she still wanted him.

"Which is why I need that security check. ASAP."

Given Walter's summation of Zara's character, which

was startlingly accurate, Zara's contention that she had left him because she didn't think he would want her in his wealthy, successful life now seemed both wimpy and implausible.

There had to be another reason.

That meant she was hiding something. Something important.

Several frantic hours later, Zara boarded Damon's private jet, carrying Rosie. A uniformed steward followed, carrying the baby bag and all of Zara's and Rosie's luggage.

Since Zara had only ever worked for Damon for a few weeks, she had never seen the jet, which was unashamedly luxurious, with spacious cabin seating and a well-appointed bathroom and sleeping cabin at the rear.

Damon stepped into the cabin, instantly dwarfing the compact space. His cool gaze briefly connected with hers, leaving her feeling oddly confused, because the warmth of that morning seemed to have disappeared. He tossed his jacket over the back of a leather seat and chatted with the steward, whose name was Mark.

Predictably, Mark was an older man with a lean, muscled physique and a somewhat grizzled face marred by what looked like a serious burn scar on one side. She had no doubt whatsoever that this was another of Damon's ex-soldiers.

As Zara tried to settle Rosie, enough that she could put the baby down to sleep in the portable crib Damon had sent ahead, the door to the flight deck popped open. Zara expected another ex-army type would have the job of pilot. Instead, a stunning blonde wearing a crisp flight uniform stepped into the cabin.

Zara continued to rock Rosie on her shoulder as the blonde introduced herself as Buffy McNamara, the pilot. Buffy lifted a hand at Damon, her polite smile transforming into a sparkling grin. Her casual "Hey, Damon" made Zara tense up inside.

Rosie chose that moment to spit up on Zara's shoulder. Feeling distracted and out of sorts, Zara searched for some baby wipes.

When Damon didn't end the conversation with Buffy, but showed every evidence of enjoying the exchange, even down to calling her Mac—the first part of her surname, and obviously some kind of extra special pet name—Zara's tension coalesced into annoyance. She was busy trying to untie Rosie's bib. What she really wanted to do was frog-march *Mac* back to the flight deck and tell her to stay there.

Jaw taut, Zara located a laundry bag and jammed the soiled bib inside it. She knew what the problem was. She was jealous, horribly jealous, although she could not afford to let Damon know that.

Damon took the seat next to her and dragged at his tie. "Is there something wrong?"

Zara found herself snared in the net of his gaze. Adrenaline zinged through her and her heart sped up.

She took a deep breath and attempted a smile. "Rosie's just a little unsettled, that's all."

At that moment Buffy strolled by on her way back to the flight deck. She paused by Damon's seat and beamed at Rosie. "Cute baby. If you need help settling her, Mark can give you a hand. In fact, you could think about moving her into the bedroom at the rear—it's quieter there and she might sleep better."

And no doubt with Rosie tidily out of sight and out of Damon's sleek, high-powered executive space, the flight would go more smoothly for the boss.

Zara fought another unreasoning spurt of annoyance. Buffy couldn't know that Rosie was Damon's daughter because they'd agreed to keep that a secret for now. "Thanks, that's a good idea, but I think Rosie will be happier here in the cabin with me."

When Buffy strode through the door of the flight deck Zara glimpsed the copilot, who *was* an older military type, just before the door closed.

Damon, his gaze tinged with amusement, offered to take Rosie. Feeling embattled, Zara handed over the baby and Rosie settled like a lamb on his shoulder.

Mark, who was busy stowing bags, looked bemused. "Hidden talents, Damon?"

"Looks like." Damon patted Rosie on the back, but he scarcely needed to because she had already fallen asleep.

Minutes later, Damon lowered Rosie into the crib and tucked a cotton blanket around her. Zara busied herself zipping the baby bag closed before stowing it beneath the seat closest to the crib. She searched through her handbag and found her phone so she could check and see if Molly, who had agreed to work full-time in the agency until Zara got back, had sent her any last-minute texts. There were none, which was a relief—

"You should come and sit down."

The low timbre of Damon's voice made her tense. She took a deep breath and tried to calm down, but despite the good talking-to she had given herself, she was still terminally annoyed at the way he had flirted with Buffy. The kind of conversation that underlined the fact that despite Rosie, despite them sleeping together *again*, she had absolutely no claim on Damon at all.

Slipping her phone back into her handbag, she took her seat and snapped open the magazine she had bought for the flight and found herself staring at a page filled with photographs of women dressed for glamorous occasions. Caroline Grant was center stage, wearing the exact same dress she had worn to the charity gala she had attended with Damon.

Zara stuffed the magazine into her bag.

"You don't have to be jealous of Mac," Damon said quietly.

Zara fastened her seat belt with a crisp click. "I'm not jealous," she muttered, keeping her voice equally low, so that Mark, who was seated at the rear of the cabin, couldn't hear. "Although I guess Buffy *is* blonde, and you do seem to have this thing for blondes."

"You're not blonde."

The jet picked up speed before leaving the ground. Zara's stomach tightened automatically as they gained height.

"And neither am I your date." She made the mistake of turning her head and was instantly ensnared by the molten silver of Damon's gaze.

"You were last night."

Heat flooded her along with a raft of memories she had been working hard to suppress and which now, literally, welded her to the seat.

"Mac is the wife of a friend. She was in the air force, part of the crew attached to our Special Forces group. She married one of the team, Brendan McNamara, which is why she goes by the nickname Mac."

Relief surged through Zara, making her feel a little shaky and ridiculously happy. Happy that Buffy/Mac was just a friend, but even happier that Damon had been considerate enough to reassure Zara. It seemed to signal another positive turn in their relationship.

"I wasn't going to do this right now," Damon murmured with an odd flatness to his voice, "but now that we're in the air and you can't walk out on me, I have a proposition for you."

Zara tensed. "A proposition?"

"As in marriage. We have a daughter. We're good

together. It won't be a marriage in the usual sense, but I think what we have is workable."

Not a marriage in the usual sense... Workable.

Zara wondered if she'd just time warped back to the nineteenth century. "Let me get this right. You're proposing a marriage—with sex—on the basis that we have a child?"

She drew a deep breath. The conditions he was offering were businesslike but more than a little hurtful. In a blinding moment of clarity she understood why. It was because a 'workable' marriage of convenience was the absolute opposite of what she wanted.

Because somehow, despite everything, she had fallen in love with Damon.

For a split second her heart seemed to stop in her chest. When it started up again, it pounded so hard she could barely breathe.

"I think you know by now that I'd like to, but I... need some time."

Because there was no way she could agree to an engagement, no matter how much she longed to. Not until he knew who she really was.

And once he knew that, he probably wouldn't want to marry her.

Ten

When Zara exited Damon's private jet, it was night. She didn't think she would be recognizable as Petra Hunt's daughter on Medinos, since it had been years since she was last here, but even so, she took precautions.

As she stepped onto the tarmac outside the terminal, she fished in her handbag and pulled out the white ball cap she had bought before boarding the flight. She had bought it expressly because it matched her white linen shirt and she could pull the bill of the cap down low over her forehead so the upper half of her face was shaded.

They stepped into the terminal and waited to clear customs. Zara relaxed a little when she noticed groups of tired tourists, a couple of people with high-visibility vests and uniformed officials, but no one resembling either a journalist or photographer.

She sent Damon a brilliant smile and tried not to notice how gorgeous and natural he looked with Rosie over his shoulder. She glanced anxiously around for their luggage. "Mark's taking a long time with the suitcases."

Damon gave her an odd look. "It's only been fifteen minutes."

Just then Mark appeared, trundling some kind of prehistoric cart with all the luggage from the flight, including that of the flight crew, who would be staying on the island until Damon and Zara were ready to fly back.

Despite the fact that it was night, it seemed to have gotten even steamier. She wiggled her toes in her white sneakers, which had been perfectly comfortable on the flight, but which were now hot and sticky.

Damon glanced at her hat as they collected their luggage. "Aren't you hot in that cap?"

Beneath the cap she was pretty sure her hair was already wet and plastered to her scalp. That was the second reason she wasn't taking it off. "It's not that hot."

"It's got to be over ninety degrees."

"I like the cap."

Damon lifted a hand to his mouth. It could have been an innocent gesture, but as Zara wheeled her case to the customs line she was pretty sure Damon had the nerve to think something about her cap was amusing. She sucked in a lungful of damp, warm air, feeling irritated because she longed to fling the blasted thing off. Her hair was already thick; the cap just added an extra sweltering layer. She caught Damon's gaze on her again as he joined her and this time she was sure he was laughing.

"I guess Rosie's going to be just like this."

"Just like *what*?"

"Frustrating. Cute."

There was a moment of vibrating silence during which Zara found it increasingly difficult to breathe. The moment was broken as the line moved forward to the customs desk. Zara dragged the hat off and quickly tried to finger comb her hair, which did feel horribly flattened and damp. The cooling relief was only momentary because a pair of dark, vaguely familiar eyes met hers. She froze like a deer caught in the headlights. Jorge—the son of her mother's gardener, Aldo—who now clearly worked for airport customs, was looking at her as if he had seen a ghost.

Before he could open his mouth and say the only name he had ever known her by—*Angel*—she shook her head. His eyes widened perceptibly, but he seemed to get the message, because his gaze swiveled to Damon.

Groaning, she kept her head down, and Jorge whisked her through customs so quickly she barely had time to look around and log the changes. The last time she had been on Medinos, the airport had been on the small side and lacking in amenities. Now it was con-

siderably larger and more complicated, with a sophis-
ticated set of duty-free shops attached.

Half an hour later, they arrived at the hotel, an old but
sumptuous building that looked like it had once been a
palace of some sort, with gorgeous tiled floors, jewel-
like water features and lavish displays of white roses
and trailing star jasmine.

The suite Damon had booked was on the sixth
floor. It was was breathtakingly luxurious, with three
bedrooms, two reception rooms, a study and a fully
equipped kitchen.

Feeling a little off balance that Damon had booked a
multiroomed suite rather than two separate suites, as if
they were already a family, Zara stowed Rosie's things
in one of the rooms. When the bellhop had gone, and
Rosie was tucked into bed, Damon opened the French
doors that led out onto a stone balcony. He threaded his
fingers with hers, sending a sharp pulse of awareness
through her as he pulled her outside.

As distracted as she was by Damon standing beside
her, muscular and relaxed in a white T-shirt and jeans,
as problematic as being on Medinos was, Zara couldn't
help but drink in the view.

The stars were out, along with a silver half-moon.
Whitewashed buildings, bleached by moonlight, with
their dark, terra-cotta tiled roofs, tumbled down to the
bay below. In the distance, she could make out the prom-
ontory, with its cluster of villas that used to be home.

Out of nowhere, her throat closed up. She hadn't

realized how much she had missed Medinos, missed having a place to truly call home. Added to that, since her mother had died, she hadn't been able to afford to come back. This would be her first opportunity to visit Petra's grave.

"It's…beautiful."

Damon plucked the cap from her head and tossed it over the balcony.

Utterly surprised, Zara yelped. She had no time to grab for the cap; all she could do was watch as it sailed down to the gardens below.

Damon tugged at her fingers, coaxing her in close. "That's better." His fingers tangled in her hair. "Your hair is too gorgeous to hide. Never wear that cap again."

Terminally annoyed, because she *needed* that cap, Zara's palms landed on his chest. Although, as annoyed as she was, a renegade part of her loved that he had pulled her close and didn't want to push him away. "That hat was *mine*."

His expression turned rueful. "I suppose you'll just go out and buy another one."

"I don't need to—I've got a spare in my suitcase."

He shrugged and released her. "Okay, wear it if you want. Just not around me."

In the instant he let her go, contrarily, she didn't want to be free. Taking the half step needed to bring her close again, she wound her arms around his neck in a loose hold.

She was aware that she was playing with fire, but she

couldn't resist. Something had changed with Damon, and she couldn't put her finger on quite what it was, except that he seemed suddenly extremely confident of her.

"I'm interested. What else am I not allowed to wear around you?"

"Clothing. Of any sort."

With a grin, Damon swept her into his arms and carried her to a sumptuous master bedroom. He tumbled her onto the very large bed, which looked like it had been made for an entire family.

A little breathlessly, Zara watched as Damon peeled out of his shirt and pants. Lit by the golden glow of a single lamp, she decided that with his broad shoulders and olive-toned skin, the black hair and tough jaw, he looked remarkably like one of the Templar knights depicted in a Medinian oil painting she had once seen.

He came down on the bed beside her and propped himself on one elbow. He ran one finger down her throat to the first button of her shirt, popping it open. "Now you."

Her breath dammed in her throat at his playful streak, which was new and unexpectedly precious because it seemed to signal the kind of intimacy she hadn't dared hope for. She climbed from the bed and began to undress, but when she got down to her bra and panties her nerve gave out, and she clambered back onto the vast bed, making up for her sudden shyness by straddling him.

Damon pulled her so that she sprawled across his chest. "That's it?"

She cupped his jaw, the clean scent of his skin making her clench her stomach. "Uh-huh. I'm not *that* experienced at this."

Damon went oddly still. "What, exactly, are you saying?"

She frowned because when they had first made love she had expected him to *know*. When he hadn't mentioned anything, she had kept the knowledge to herself because the relationship was so new and she hadn't wanted him to think she was trying to tie him to her.

Before she could actually say it, he muttered something short and flat beneath his breath. "You were a virgin."

She traced the line of his mouth with the pad of her thumb and tried to make light of it She hadn't consciously set out to stay a virgin; she had just never met anyone she actually wanted to make love with until Damon. Petra's death and the problems with the media hadn't helped. Zara had basically retreated into her shell and stayed there.

She shrugged. "It doesn't matter now. But I'm glad that you know." Then, even if the worst happened and he hated her for being Petra's daughter, he would at least know that the tabloids had lied about her.

He caught her fingers in his and pulled them to his lips. "I'm sorry I missed that moment, babe. But I'm glad you've only ever been mine."

Babe. Happiness seemed to expand inside her as he rolled so that she was beneath him. But despite the heat that shimmered through her, despite the coiling tension that was already making it hard to breathe, let alone think, a tiny thought niggled. "What about you?"

Damon had dispensed with her bra, now he cupped her breasts, his palms faintly abrasive against her tender skin. His thumbs swept across her nipples, making it difficult to concentrate on what was, suddenly, a very important question.

His gaze captured hers. "What do you mean, what about me?"

She drew in a sharp breath as he took the nipple of one breast into his mouth. "I mean, Caroline."

Damon moved and she lifted her hips to assist him as he peeled down her panties. "Remember that reporter who came to your office?"

Zara drew in a sharp breath as Damon parted her legs with his thigh. She tried to think, but with his muscular weight now pressing her down into the mattress, her normally excellent memory had deserted her. "Um…Red Glasses."

Damon grinned and rewarded her with a kiss, which sent a ridiculously happy glow through her.

"Vanessa Gardiner. She was a friend of Caroline's. Why do you think Caroline put a reporter on my tail?"

Zara tried to gather her thoughts, but with the enticing pressure between her legs and the heated ache low in her belly, it was difficult to think of anything but how long it was going to take Damon to actually start making love to her. "I give up."

Damon's darkened gaze pinned her. "Caroline wanted to know who I was sleeping with."

Understanding finally dawned. "Because you weren't sleeping with her." She swallowed, feeling suddenly, unexpectedly teary. "That means—"

"I haven't slept with anyone else."

Feeling just the tiniest bit fierce and possessive, she coiled her arms around his neck and pulled him close, relieved when he finally began entering her. When he was fully sheathed, she wrapped her legs around his hips, trying to pull him closer still.

She thought she had already felt everything she was going to feel with Damon, that nothing could be more intense and more meaningful than the lovemaking they had already shared. But as they began making slow, exquisite love to each other she discovered she had been wrong.

The knowledge that he had been celibate for the last thirteen months changed things. It made the deep, lasting love she craved with Damon seem possible. As she kissed him back, touched him back, with every breath, suddenly the night was alive with emotions that shimmered and burned, melded and entwined...

Zara awoke to sun streaming through the French doors and Rosie patting her cheek. A little startled that she had slept so late and that Damon had taken charge of Rosie, Zara shifted up in the bed, pulling the linen sheets around her breasts as she cuddled her daughter.

Damon looked gorgeous in light jeans and a white T-shirt, his phone to one ear. He terminated the call, bent down and kissed her on the mouth.

"Stay in bed and rest. I'm driving out to the house to talk to Ben. Rosie's had her breakfast, so if you like, I can take her with me. I'll only be a couple of hours at most, and Mark ordered a car with tinted windows and a car seat, so she'll be safe *and* incognito."

Zara watched, a faint lump in her throat, as Damon strapped on the front pack and neatly fitted a gurgling Rosie into the cushioned frame. He seemed to be an expert at the fatherhood thing already. But she was all too aware after Damon's revelation and the fact that they seemed poised on the brink of a real relationship that the bubble of happiness she was presently living in could burst at any moment.

She needed to tell Damon the truth today.

Zara showered and dressed in an ice-blue dress that made the most of her tan. Humming beneath her breath, she sat at the exquisite antique dressing table to do her hair. As she coiled the heavy, glossy strands into a knot on top of her head and began sliding in pins, she couldn't help noticing that she looked *different*. She had heard women speak of glowing when they were in love. She was glowing. Her eyes were alight, her skin radiant, her mouth softly curved.

She applied minimal makeup, fitted earrings and

did a final check of her appearance. She had a floppy-brimmed hat to wear, but at the last minute decided she was over the hat idea. She dragged a pair of large sunglasses out of her handbag instead. *Good!* With the sunglasses hiding her eyes and her cheekbones, she barely recognized herself.

She checked her watch. Damon wouldn't be long. If she was going to visit Petra's grave, see her mother's lawyer, then go to the bank to see what, exactly, Petra had stashed in the safe-deposit box—if anything—she needed to hurry.

She bought an armful of pretty flowers from a street vendor, then took a taxi to the local cemetery, which was situated on the windblown side of a hill overlooking the sea. Finding Petra's grave was easy, because she was buried near the ancient stone chapel, right beside Zara's father. Chest tight, her throat locked, Zara gently laid the flowers down. She hadn't quite known how she was going to feel, but there was a wild beauty about the hillside and the stone cross of the chapel etched against blue sky, a curious sense of peace and closure.

A few minutes later, the taxi delivered her to the address on the last letter she had received from her mother's legal firm. The white limestone building was situated on one of the steep, narrow streets that were a feature of Medinos.

She stepped out of the glaring heat of the sun into the inky well of shade offered by the foyer. She stopped by the front desk, and the receptionist, who was on a call, put the phone down. Before she could show Zara to Takis's office, a plump, balding man with a rumpled suit stepped out of a door.

The receptionist spoke in rapid Medinian. Zara heard her own name and realized she was looking at her mother's lawyer.

Takis stared at her for a long moment. "You do not look like your mother."

Tell me about it. "Nevertheless, I am Petra Hunt's daughter."

He held his door open with discernible reluctance. Jaw set, Zara walked into the small, rather messy office.

"Please, take a seat. What can I do for you?"

"I would like to view my mother's file."

"You know she signed the prenuptial—"

"I'm not worried about that." She attempted a smooth smile. "It's the offer by the McCall estate that I'm really interested in."

Takis frowned. "I don't understand. I sent you a copy—"

"I burned it."

There was a moment of taut silence. Takis walked to a wall of files, searched for what seemed an age before pulling out a folder. The chair behind his desk squeaked as he sat down. He flipped open the file, turned it around and pushed it across the desk toward her.

Zara skimmed the document, turned a page and froze. Damon's signature seemed to leap off the page. When she had originally received the offer, she hadn't paid much attention to the signature. Since then, a part of her had hoped it hadn't been Damon who had signed it, that it actually had been some faceless lawyer.

"May I have a copy of this?"

Minutes later, still feeling numb because Damon had been the architect of that horrible offer after all, Zara strolled down the steep street and into the bustling center of Medinos. The midday heat poured down as she crossed at a busy intersection, thronged with holiday-makers, but she barely noticed the swarms of brightly colored tourists.

Feeling suddenly thirsty, she stopped at a small café and bought one of Medinos's signature drinks, an enticing cordial of plum and lemon poured over shaved ice that quickly dissolved in the heat.

The bank her mother had used was easy enough to find. An entirely new tension hummed through her as she took in the high-vaulted ceilings, plaster frescoes and elegant marble floor. A pretty bank clerk directed her to an office that opened off the reception area. A trim, darkly suited clerk checked Zara's ID and the copy of Petra's will she had brought with her before escorting her down an echoing corridor. He entered a code into a thoroughly modern keypad and waited for her to precede him into another room.

A guard seated at a desk asked to see her key. He took note of the number and disappeared into an adjacent room. Seconds later, he appeared with a key, then opened a steel door into the vault and indicated she fol-

low him. Zara watched as he unlocked a steel compart-
ment and pulled out a long, narrow steel box, which he
laid on a small table. Nodding politely, he withdrew,
leaving her in privacy to unlock the box.

Out of nowhere, her heart began to pound.

When her mother had died, Zara had been thousands
of miles away and had not had the funds to get back for
the funeral. A model friend of her mother's had packed
up Petra's things and freighted them to Zara. Opening
those boxes and sorting through her mother's clothes
and personal effects had been the only ritual left to her.
That was possibly why she was now unbearably aware
that the last time this safe-deposit box had been opened,
it had been by her mother.

Petra had stood in this same sterile room while she
placed whatever it was that she had held most precious
in the narrow steel box. Emotion swelled in Zara's
chest—a sudden, powerful sense of connection with
the mother she had lost, emotions she had avoided because losing Petra had cut the ground from under her.
Despite their differences they had always been a pair—
two against the world.

Taking a deep breath, she inserted the key, turned it
and opened the box. She instantly recognized the faded
leather cases that held Atrides family jewelry; she had
seen them often enough as a child. After lifting them
out, she opened them, emotion swelling as she looked at
the pretty collection of French brooches and pendants,

the huge old-fashioned cameo her great-grandmother had worn with a black bombazine dress.

Her fingers brushed against a small black velvet bag. She loosened the cord and emptied the contents into the palm of her hand. Not jewelry as she had expected, but a glittering cascade of diamonds; single stones of varying sizes, all of them glowing with an expensive fire.

Once, over a glass of wine, Petra had alluded to her *life savings*. She hadn't said what the savings were exactly. Zara had thought she was talking about money, but the amount in Petra's bank accounts had been too small to qualify as savings of any sort. Now she knew that her mother had been referring to this cache of diamonds, her hedge against the hard times that would come when her looks faded.

Heart thumping, she poured the diamonds into the pouch like so much liquid fire and carefully retied the cord. Her mother hadn't lived long enough to need the money the diamonds would bring. But Zara was certain Petra would love it that her *savings* would be put to good use, and not just for a deposit on a house—she would buy the whole thing.

The final items in the box were a plain white envelope, a solitaire engagement ring, a gold wedding ring worn thin over the years and a silver cross that she recognized as once belonging to her father.

Zara's throat closed up as she extracted the jewelry that had been the intimate, personal belongings of her parents. She had wondered what had happened to her mother's rings, which Petra was usually never without. She had assumed they had been lost in the accident somehow, or maybe misplaced by the people who had sorted through Petra's things.

Frowning, Zara opened the last item, the envelope, and extracted a sheaf of what looked like certificates. Her heart seemed to stop in her chest as the name *McCall Electrical* jumped out at her. Stunned, Zara flipped through a sheaf of numbered shares in McCall Electrical. Voting shares, the shares Damon had been chasing for the past year or so and which had blocked his takeover bid of the company. Shares that Tyler must have gifted to Petra and which now, technically, belonged to Zara.

With careful precision, because her fingers were shaking, she placed the certificates on the table. From her work on the McCall deal, Zara knew they represented a 10 percent chunk of McCall Electrical, which meant they were worth tens of millions of dollars.

Suddenly, her aunt Phoebe's motives in placing Zara at Damon's business made an even more horrible kind of sense. Her aunt must have known about the existence of the shares and their value. She had obviously hoped that if Zara got to know Damon before she found out about the shares, that she wouldn't reject them as she'd rejected the cash offer by Damon.

"Sorry, Phoebe," Zara muttered beneath her breath. "You should have known you were wasting your time. I wouldn't touch these with a barge pole."

As far as she was concerned, they belonged to

Damon and Ben; she wanted no part of them. She stared at the shares, feeling suddenly utterly panicked. It was bad enough that she had to explain her true identity to Damon; having to explain the shares was too much.

First off, if she gave the shares back to Damon, he would know that her mother had had them, which would confirm his opinion of Petra and make him doubly suspicious of Zara. Second, she was almost certain that Damon would view her gesture as calculated. He was a billionaire and had already proposed marriage, so financially she would not need the shares. Whichever way she looked at it, giving the shares back to Damon herself could mean he would no longer want marriage with her, and she could not risk that.

She would have to find a way to get them back to Damon so that he would never know she'd had them all along.

Last night she had seen a glimmer of what the future could hold for them. She couldn't bear it if he rejected her outright. She loved him, and she wanted him to love her. With the shares in her possession, more than ever, she needed to pick the right time to tell him. Although, she was beginning to wonder if such a moment existed.

Hating even to touch shares that she would rather die than accept, Zara shoved them back into the envelope. As she did so, she noticed a slip of paper. It was a note written from Tyler to Petra in a clean, slanting hand. In essence it said that because Petra had insisted on a prenuptial agreement and refused to share in his wealth and assets, he insisted she accept the shares, which were an engagement present.

Knees feeling wobbly, Zara sat down. Her spine and scalp were tingling, all the fine hairs at her nape raised, her chest tight. The words Tyler had written were straightforward and businesslike, but Tyler giving Petra stock in his firm could mean only one thing, just as Petra taking off the wedding rings Zara's father had given her could mean only one thing.

They had been deeply in love.

Zara's fingers closed automatically over the thin wedding band and the pretty solitaire diamond. Petra had loved Zara's father to the point that no man had ever lived up to him. Even after his death, she had worn his rings and had never consented to wearing anyone else's jewelry. Zara had known that, because as a child, worrying about who might replace her father, she had come to realize that as long as Petra wore her wedding ring, there would be no replacement. Every time Petra had visited her at school, or taken her away on holiday, the first thing Zara had done was check her mother's left hand. Despite all the speculative media reports about who Petra was dating, if she was still wearing her wedding rings, that meant their small family of two was still intact.

Zara reread the note Tyler had written, and this time she noticed the date. Two days before Petra and Tyler had died.

Petra had been engaged. Her relationship had been real and valid. The shares proved that.

The shares.

Zara felt like flinging them somewhere, *burning them*, but she couldn't do either thing. She was caught between a rock and a hard place, because Damon needed the shares to gain control of McCall Electrical.

Feverishly, she tossed Tyler's note onto the table while she examined the envelope itself. It was plain and white, with no writing on it. Good. She would find a way to have the shares delivered to Damon, maybe pay someone to drop them off at the concierge desk. It had to be someone she trusted, yet who couldn't be connected to her.

Feeling like a cat on hot bricks—elated because the diamonds represented the financial security she and Rosie desperately needed, and utterly stressed at finding the missing McCall shares—she gathered everything from the table and shoved it all into her bag.

She had hoped she would recover some family jewelry today, and she had; what she hadn't expected was for the past to rush back at her like a freight train. A past she had to explain to Damon so he wouldn't end up hating her.

Above all, she didn't want him to think the reason she was so attracted to him had anything to do with his money. It wasn't true and it would never be true. What she wanted was what she had always wanted, to be loved and cherished for herself.

Pushing to her feet, she hooked the strap of her bag over her shoulder and checked her watch. Anxiety made her stomach hollow when she saw how much time had passed. Almost an hour, although it had felt like a lot less.

After handing in her key because she wouldn't be needing the box again, she made a beeline back to the main foyer of the bank. As she stepped out onto the pavement, the glare of the afternoon sun had her rummaging for her sunglasses. Sliding them onto the bridge of her nose, she hailed a cab. Relieved when the cab veered toward her, she slid into the back seat and gave the cabbie the hotel's address, suddenly anxious to get back to Rosie.

Five minutes later, the cab stopped at the hotel entrance. After paying the fare, Zara stepped into the foyer. She stopped dead when she saw Emily, who was sitting in one of the leather chairs, watching the entrance and clearly waiting for her.

"What's wrong?"

Emily dragged Zara toward the most secluded couch, positioned beneath a lush indoor palm right next to the elevators. "Damon's talking to Ben." Her face crumpled. "At first I thought Damon was okay with Ben and I being together, then Walter called, and everything changed. We had to come here because the cell phone coverage is practically nonexistent out on the coast and Walter had emailed some kind of report—"

"An investigative report."

Emily's face went white. "I think so, because Ben knows about Daniel now."

Zara took the seat next to Emily. "Daniel? I thought his name was Jason."

Emily flushed. "I guessed by now you would know too. Daniel was before Jason. He was a business partner of my father's. My father wanted me to marry him. I liked him quite a lot—I even thought I might be in love with him—so I agreed, but then I met Jason."

"So you pulled out of the marriage."

She shrugged. "I fell for Jason. He could have been a pauper for all I cared."

"But he wasn't. He was even richer, so it made you look like you were chasing a bigger catch."

Emily looked miserable. "I thought I'd made the right choice until Jason dumped me. Unfortunately, when it happened some columnist wrote a snarky piece about it, accusing me of bed-hopping and chasing a rich husband. I felt so humiliated, I left my job in my father's business—"

"Changed your name and came to work for me."

Emily flushed. "You seem so calm about this. I thought you'd be steaming mad. I thought you'd hate me." She grimaced. "Just like Ben will. I'm pretty sure Walter will have dug up that horrible article."

Abruptly, the fear that had been sawing at Zara ever since she'd discovered the shares died and was replaced by an odd sense of calm. If Walter had investigated Emily, then he would be investigating her, which meant she was out of time. She grimly wondered if Damon had also received a security report about her.

The last few days, her life had been tipped upside down and spun around and, quite frankly, she was over the stress of it. She was a good person. She loved her daughter and she loved Damon and she wanted to share her life with him. But if he preferred security reports and the rubbish the media invented over her word, then she was out of options.

A painful flush suffused Emily's face. "Damon's very protective of Ben. I can understand why he would want to warn him off—"

"Ben's an adult," she said crisply. "He doesn't need his older brother interfering in something that is none of his business."

Emily looked startled. "I thought you'd be furious, which is why I wanted to catch you before you spoke to Damon. It was bad enough that I walked out on my job—" She fumbled in her handbag, found a tissue and blew her nose. "I've made a real mess of things. I don't even know if Ben will ever let me explain—"

The elevator doors opened. Ben strode out, his face pale, his expression taut. His gaze zeroed in on Emily.

"You're still here," he muttered. "Thank goodness. I thought you would have run a mile."

Emily jumped to her feet. "Why would I run?"

"Because my family's so messed up. Why would you want to be a part of us? I've just heard it all. My father was a crazy, violent drunk and a womanizer who squandered the family fortune on mistresses. I was born after he died, so I never knew him, but Damon did, and he's literally got the scars to prove it. That's why he's so...overprotective. He doesn't want me falling into the same pit of snakes." Ben grinned lopsidedly.

Emily looked devastated. "He thinks I'm a pit of snakes?"

Ben instantly clasped her upper arms and pulled her close, his expression anxious. "Baby, that came out all wrong. The pit of snakes is the out-of-control, addictive behavior Damon thinks runs in the family line, not you."

"Phew," Emily said, with the glimmer of a watery smile. "For a moment there I thought Damon must hate me."

"Damon doesn't hate anyone. He just doesn't want me to get hurt."

Emily stiffened. "And do *you* think I'll hurt you?"

"Only if you leave me."

"I wasn't intending to leave. Why would I? I love you."

Relief washed over Ben's face. "Ditto. I don't care about your past relationships, and the truth is I've hardly been an altar boy myself, if you know what I mean. If you're happy with me, that's all I want to know."

Emily threw Zara a radiant glance as Ben hurried her out of the hotel. "Sorry about the job, Zara, but it looks like I'm definitely not coming back!"

Zara watched as Ben settled Emily into a low-slung

sports car, which was parked just across the road. Feeling a little stunned by what Ben had revealed about Damon's past, Zara made a beeline toward the elevators.

Damon having a father who had driven the family broke with his spending on mistresses neatly explained his attitude toward Petra, and to Angel Atrides. It also made sense of his attempt to pay her off and get her to sign that insulting "go away" agreement. Ben had also mentioned scars, and that their father had been violent. She had always thought Damon's scars had been earned in battle, but some of them must have been inflicted by his father.

Slowly, quietly, the pieces of the puzzle fell into place and her heart squeezed tight at what Damon must have endured as a child. She was beginning to understand why he had such an issue with trust.

As the elevator whizzed upward, her stomach tensed. Emily's expression had glowed; she had gotten her happy ending. An ending Zara now very much doubted would be hers.

When she stepped into the suite, Rosie, who was lying on a rug on the floor playing with a rattle, crowed, flung the toy aside and held her arms out to Zara. A rush of pure maternal love brought tears to Zara's eyes. It might not be possible that she could ever have the true, adult love she needed from Damon, but she had her daughter.

Zara carried her handbag, with all of its incriminating evidence, into Rosie's room and stashed it in a dark corner. She walked back out to the sitting room and scooped Rosie up, needing the comfort of her child in her arms.

Damon strolled out of the adjoining study, a cell in his hand. Zara decided to take the bull by the horns. "I saw Emily and Ben in the lobby. Luckily, Ben had the maturity to see beyond Emily's past to what a nice person she is."

Damon dropped the phone into his back pocket. "I agree that Emily is nice," he said mildly. "But if she had been up-front about her past to begin with, there wouldn't have been a problem."

"Maybe Emily had some very good reasons for keeping her life, and her name, private."

"Most people don't deal with it by changing their name."

Zara stared at Damon for a long moment, wondering if there was a double meaning to his words because he knew she had changed her name. Rosie, who had slumped into a contented doze almost as soon as Zara had picked her up, stirred, as if even in sleep she could sense the uncomfortable currents. "You say that as if she did it to deliberately deceive Ben, when all she wanted was to escape the press and keep her privacy."

Damon frowned. "The press were not exactly hounding Emily. As I recall, it was one gossip columnist."

"Just one? Then Emily can't have been that notorious." Afraid that she would lose her temper and reveal too much, Zara walked through to Rosie's room, placed her in her crib and covered her with a light cotton blanket. She drew a deep breath and discovered that her hands were shaking. The one ray of hope was that, given that they were still talking about Emily, maybe Damon hadn't yet received a report about her.

When she walked out to the sitting room, Damon's gaze was wary. "What have I done now?"

He was standing at a set of French doors that opened out onto a sun-drenched patio. With his arms crossed over his chest, making his shoulders seem even broader, he looked brooding, utterly masculine and more than a little dangerous.

Zara got straight to the point. "Emily said you got Walter to dig into her past."

"Ben's my brother. He's in love with a woman who, at some point, changed her name." He shrugged. "Of course, I got Walter to do a little digging—"

"I suppose you think Emily's not good enough for Ben?"

Damon's brows jerked together. "These days what I think doesn't really impact Ben."

But it impacted Zara! "Okay, then, *you* don't think Emily's good enough."

Damon reached her in two strides. Linking his fingers with hers, he pulled her close, which was disorienting when she was still bracing herself for the fact that he had received some kind of damning report on her.

"Forget Emily," he muttered. "I had hoped we might be doing something else right about now."

The bell to the suite buzzed. Damon swore softly. "Talk about bad timing."

He opened the door to a waiter, who wheeled in a cart with a bottle of champagne on ice and two glasses. Damon tipped the waiter and closed the door behind him before wheeling the cart off to one side.

His expression was rueful. "I was supposed to give you something before that happened."

He fished a velvet box out of his pocket and flipped the lid. For a split second she thought he had an engagement ring, then she saw a pair of gorgeous diamond earrings.

For a moment she battled disappointment, then the sheer relief that Damon still wanted to give her a gift, and the sheer beauty of the earrings, took over.

Despite his contention that he wanted to keep things on a businesslike footing, he had obviously been thinking about her and wanting to please her, even down to doing something romantic like ordering champagne. A lump formed in her throat as it occurred to her that, even though everything seemed to be happening in reverse—as in having sex and a baby!—Damon was now courting her.

"You don't have to give me jewelry—"

"After last night, I wanted you to have something."

Understanding dawned. Last night she had told him that she had only ever been his.

Fingers shaking slightly, she picked up the gorgeous earrings, walked over to the mirror and inserted them in her lobes. She had been about to say that she couldn't accept them, but now she didn't want to let them go because she was certain they were a genuine gift of love, even if Damon didn't realize it.

"They're...beautiful."

Damon came up behind her and pulled her back against the warmth of his chest. "You're beautiful."

He turned her around in his arms and kissed her. Zara wound her arms around his neck and kissed him back, happiness shimmering through her as she wallowed in the sheer warmth and comfort of being back in Damon's arms, but the moment was bittersweet. As wonderful as it was to just be with Damon, to let her imagination run riot and pretend that they were both in love, it was a fact that they were on borrowed time.

And she had the sudden premonition that if she didn't make love to Damon now, she never would again.

A little feverishly, she began undoing the buttons of his shirt.

Damon lifted his head, his gaze heated. "Now?"

For an answer, she kissed him again and dragged at more buttons. Damon's shirt dropped to the floor. This time he pulled her close and kissed her. Long drugging seconds later her dress followed suit and she found herself propelled in the direction of the bedroom.

Damon kicked the bedroom door closed behind them as they stepped through. By the time they reached the bed, Damon had stepped out of his pants and her bra was gone. There was a momentary pause while Damon sheathed himself with a condom then they were lying tangled together on the sun-drenched bed.

She felt the glide of Damon's fingers as he peeled her panties down her legs. Desire shivered and burned as he came down between her thighs. With one smooth thrust he was inside her and they were deeply, perfectly linked.

Damon's gaze locked with hers and his fierce tenderness struck her to the heart. For a split second, she felt the utter rightness of being together, that he truly belonged to her and she to him.

She clasped his shoulders as they began to move, tears blinding her at the sheer intimacy of what they were doing. She felt as if she was finally, truly getting to know Damon and at the same time saying goodbye.

Eleven

Damon woke to small noises signaling that Rosie was awake. Carefully, so as not to disturb Zara, he disentangled himself, slid from the bed and pulled on his jeans. Walking into Rosie's room, he found her cuddle rug, which was lying on the floor, then looked around for her favorite toy, a rattle, which had also ended up on the floor. As he picked up the rattle, he noticed Zara's white leather handbag, which was lying at a drunken angle between an armchair and the wall with her phone precariously balanced on top. Probably in a rush to put Rosie in the crib, she had simply dumped the lot.

He handed the rattle to Rosie, who instantly started to chew on it, then retrieved Zara's phone. As he did so, the bag, which seemed stuffed full, slumped to one side. A number of items spilled out on the floor, among them a black velvet bag that scattered brilliant crystals. Jaw tight, Damon stooped to gather up gems that burned with the fiery, unmistakable glitter of diamonds.

He was no expert, but given the size, number and weight of the stones, he was looking at a small fortune. He tipped the stones back into the velvet bag and placed it in Zara's handbag. As he did so, he noticed a thick envelope, which had also fallen out of the bag. The envelope was plain, but the contents, which had partly slid out of the envelope, looked gut-wrenchingly familiar. He picked up the envelope, already knowing what he was going to find. Even so, his stomach contracted when he pulled out the sheaf of old-fashioned and utterly familiar share certificates.

The missing McCall shares.

Why would Zara have the shares in her possession? How had she gotten hold of them?

The only answer that made sense was that Zara was somehow connected with Tyler. Because the voting shares were supposed to be held only by family members, he had considered the possibility that Tyler had given them to Petra, then on Petra's death they had ended up in Angel's hands. But the shares had never appeared on the market, so he had scrapped that idea.

It suddenly occurred to him that Zara was the same age as Petra's daughter, Angel Atrides. It was a leap—a big one. She looked nothing like Petra, but the more he thought about it, the more the facts fitted. It explained why Zara was so sensitive about any contact with the press, and why she had been so protective of Emily changing her name.

He had a sudden flash of Zara's bedroom, which had been decorated in a distinctly Medinian way and suddenly he was sure.

Zara Westlake was Angel Atrides.

It was there in the mystery about Zara's *nondisclosure*, the fact that she had gotten passports for her and Rosie, and had been surprisingly willing to come to Medinos. If he didn't miss his guess, Petra had stored the diamonds and the share certificates at some bank, and Zara had needed to come to Medinos personally to retrieve them.

Keeping hold of the envelope, Damon rose to his feet. He felt as if the scales had fallen from his eyes. He had been bedazzled, incapable of operating with his usual methodical precision.

A little grimly, he wondered if this was how Tyler had felt when he had fallen for Petra and handed over the shares of a business that had been his life's work. A company he had built up with clever innovation and long hours of hard work. A company he had always maintained would remain in the family.

A soft buzzing distracted Damon. He retrieved his phone from the back pocket of his jeans. Walter's text advised Damon that the report on Zara was in his inbox and he needed to read it before he did something stupid.

Too late. Damon walked to the study and used his

laptop to read the confirmation that Zara Westlake was Angel Atrides.

Picking up the envelope that contained the shares, he walked back to the bedroom as Zara's eyes flickered open.

The words Ben had spoken over the phone just before he had flown away with Emily came back to haunt Damon. He lacked *emotional intelligence.*

He had no argument with that summation. He had ignored his usual caution and allowed himself to be conned by Petra's daughter.

It had all been a sham from the first moment.

He dropped the envelope on the pillow. Some of the shares slipped out, fanning across the tangled sheet. He saw the comprehension in Zara's gaze and the cold in his stomach seemed to settle a little deeper.

"How did you get hold of the shares?"

Zara jackknifed, clutching the sheet around her breasts. "You searched my bag?"

"I didn't search anything. I went in to check on Rosie. I noticed you'd left your phone on top of your bag. When I picked it up your bag fell over and a few things you obviously didn't want me to see fell out."

"It's not what you think." She averted her gaze from the certificates. "They were in a safe-deposit box at my mother's bank."

"Which was why you wanted to come to Medinos."

"I didn't know the stock certificates were there!"

"What about the diamonds?"

"Not those, either! I came because I wanted to find out what was in the box. I had hoped my Atrides family jewelry would be there, and it was."

"Atrides, as in Angel Atrides."

Her gaze turned fierce. "That's right. I changed my name for practical reasons—"

"Like Emily."

"I did it to escape the media. Not that I would expect you to understand that!"

"And the small fortune in diamonds didn't really matter?"

"Actually, *yes*, it does, because right now Rosie and I need the money. To be honest, I was *glad* there were diamonds."

"Not that you need the diamonds, with the shares being worth a small fortune."

Her face went white. "I told you I didn't know the certificates were there. I didn't know any of it was there!"

Damon's jaw tightened. "Just like you didn't know when you slept with me that I was Tyler's nephew?"

"You think I slept with you and got pregnant, *deliberately*?" Zara clambered from the bed and dragged on one of the hotel robes, belting it tight. "You're wrong about my mother, and you're wrong about me! My aunt Phoebe pulled some strings to help get me the job. And, yes, *she* had an agenda, but she didn't let me in on it! If I had known which Smith you were, I wouldn't have taken the job—I wouldn't have touched you with a barge pole—"

"I can't believe you didn't know who I was."

"Your name is Smith. Do you know how many people have that surname? The firm is Magnum Security, which I had never heard of before. It wasn't until I started working on the McCall takeover that it finally clicked that you were *that* Smith."

Damon dragged lean fingers through his hair. He couldn't believe how much he wanted to believe her. "Maybe if the shares weren't involved—"

"Tyler gave those shares to my mother because he *loved* her."

"And you have proof of this?" Damon couldn't keep the sardonic twist from his mouth. Although there was no humor in a situation that took him straight back to his childhood and his father's penchant for lavishing expensive gifts on his mistresses.

Zara shot him a fiery glance. "You think you have all the facts, but you don't. My mother wouldn't agree to marry Tyler without a prenup, because she didn't want his money. Tyler agreed, but in return, he insisted she take shares in his company. I can prove it. There was a note from Tyler in the safe-deposit box."

Damon's expression was utterly neutral. "Sounds like true love."

"It was. My mother took off her wedding rings. If you had known her at all, you would have known what that meant, because she adored my father and grieved him for years. Until she met Tyler she never took off her rings. But you didn't know Petra, just like you don't know me."

Damon followed Zara as she marched into Rosie's room, found her bag, carried it out to the sitting room and feverishly searched through it. When she couldn't find what she was looking for she began emptying items onto the coffee table. After a few minutes, she quietly repacked her bag.

"No note?"

Frustration brimmed in her gaze. "I must have left it in the vault. Although you won't believe that because you think I'm lying."

He frowned. "I didn't say that."

"I've told you what happened," she said flatly, "but I don't think you want the truth. You'd rather see me as flawed and dishonorable, because if you were convinced that I was genuine, then that might demand some kind of genuine response from you, and that's something you don't want to give. What happened a year ago is a case in point. I left and you didn't come after me."

"I did," he said quietly. "And I found you, but I left before you saw me."

Her expression was oddly stricken. "That's even worse."

Zara marched back to the bedroom, gathered up the shares and shoved them back into their envelope. She remembered the earrings Damon had given her and which she was still wearing! Fingers shaking, she fumbled the earrings out of her lobes, located the box they had come in, then placed the jewelry box on the coffee table with the shares.

"The shares are yours—I don't want them. You can have the earrings back, as well. Consider yourself freed."

Silence seemed to stretch between them, hollow and unbridgeable.

Damon's phone buzzed. Turning on his heel, he walked back into the study and closed the door.

Moving on automatic pilot, Zara made it to the bathroom and locked the door behind her. Feeling sick to her stomach, she stared blankly at her reflection in the lavish mirror, which occupied most of one wall. Taking a deep, slow breath that hurt because her chest was tight with misery, she noted that, with her hair a wild tangle around her face and the robe gaping slightly over her breasts, she looked lush and wanton. The complete opposite of the woman she knew herself to be.

Although, Damon could not seem to see *her*.

Suddenly unable to bear looking at herself, she dropped the robe on the floor and stepped beneath the shower. She winced as cool water struck her skin. As the water gradually warmed, her numbness faded and the decision she knew she had to make settled into place.

She had to leave. Now.

She could not afford to argue with Damon anymore.

If she did, she would end up begging, and she absolutely did not want to beg.

She loved him, but it was clear that Damon did not love her. Not even close. The death knell had been when he admitted that a year ago he had found her and *then walked away.*

If he had truly wanted her, he would have pursued her back then, and he would be fighting for her now, just like Ben had fought for Emily. But Damon was clearly more interested in pushing her out of his life than holding on to her.

She didn't blame him for being angry or distrustful, because she had hardly engendered his trust. She should have told Damon who she was a long time ago. She had been guilty of cowardice, guilty of running away, but it was also a fact that some things had just happened.

Their relationship had been fatally flawed from the beginning, but it had resulted in Rosie, who was gorgeous and lovable and who Zara could never regret having. To Zara's mind there was nothing that was not forgivable between her and Damon. The problem was that Damon did not trust in love. And the very strength she had found so attractive in him had ended up finishing them.

Minutes later, dried and with the robe once more belted around her middle, she opened the door and listened. Reassured by the silence that pervaded the suite that Damon had left, she walked quickly to the bedroom. A quick peek at Rosie told her that she had fallen back to sleep.

Zara dressed quickly in cotton jeans, a camisole and an airy white shirt. Leaving her hair loose, she used minimal makeup and slipped on comfortable sandals.

Her stomach churned as she quickly packed, but she knew it was the right thing to do. She could not stay with a man who felt contempt for her, no matter how wrong she knew his attitude to be.

She checked the bedside clock. Barely fifteen minutes had passed since she had stepped out of the shower. She didn't know how much time she had before Damon came back to the suite. All she knew was that after their horrible confrontation, she couldn't bear to see him again.

In her haste, she emptied an entire drawer into her suitcase, not bothering to fold or be neat. She remembered to grab her toiletries from the bathroom, shoving them into a plastic bag so nothing would leak.

She collected Rosie's bag and stuffed in clothes, bottles, baby formula and diapers. After making up a bottle, she zipped the bag closed with difficulty and deposited it, along with the folded front pack, in the tray below the baby stroller. After letting the backrest of the stroller down so that it formed a bed, Zara gingerly deposited Rosie in the stroller and tucked her cotton blanket around her. Rosie blinked sleepily.

Relieved, Zara checked the bedroom and the sitting room. She would not be able to take all of Rosie's equipment with her; the portable crib and the bedding that went with it would have to stay behind.

Zara wheeled her suitcase to the door and collected her handbag. She stopped dead when she checked inside to make sure she had her sunglasses and noticed the bag of diamonds jumbled in among the Atrides jewelry cases. No doubt Damon had thought all the wrong things about her when he had seen them, along with the share certificates.

Tucking the jewelry cases and the diamonds in the bottom of her suitcase, she looped the strap of her handbag over one shoulder, wheeled her suitcase out into the hall, then wheeled the stroller out. She tensed as she walked toward the elevator, pushing the stroller with one hand and wheeling the suitcase along behind her with the other. She didn't know where Damon had gone, but she was aware that he could return at any time. She punched the call button for the elevator. When the doors slid open to reveal an empty car, she breathed a sigh of relief.

She pushed the stroller in and turned it around and managed to drag the suitcase in beside her just before the doors closed. She pushed the ground floor button, then slid sunglasses onto the bridge of her nose.

As she struggled out of the elevator, she automatically scanned the foyer. There was a group of tourists checking out, their luggage attended by two bellhops. A couple sat in the sleek lounge area and, across an expanse of marble floor, the café and bar was filled with tourists enjoying the thick aromatic local coffee.

Heart still beating too rapidly, Zara made a beeline for the door.

When the concierge started toward her, a frown on his face, she fell back into the training she had received at her finishing school and politely smiled as she shook her head. Dismissed, the concierge retreated and, with a weakening sense of relief, she made it through the doors to the first taxi.

She tipped the driver double what she expected to pay for the fare after he folded up the stroller and stowed it in the trunk, and asked him to drive her to the law firm. The driver waited for her while she took Rosie into the office. Fifteen minutes later, Zara exited the building with a baby who was now distinctly unhappy, but she had the document she needed, signed and witnessed by the receptionist.

Sliding into the back seat of the taxi, she rummaged in the baby bag and found the bottle of formula she had prepared. Popping it into Rosie's mouth, she asked the taxi driver to take her back to the hotel, but to park down a side street where she could walk through the hotel café to the foyer. That way she could get into the hotel without the exposure of parking at the front entrance.

With no alternative but to take Rosie with her, she asked the driver to wait once more, tipping him to make sure he didn't drive off with her luggage. Jamming the almost empty bottle back into the baby bag, she exited the taxi and walked into the hotel through the busy café, pausing before the open expanse of the foyer, just in case by some chance Damon might be walking through.

When the coast seemed clear, she walked briskly to the concierge's desk and asked that the document be delivered to Damon's suite.

Damon walked into the vault of the third and final bank on Medinos. He'd had to call in some favors, but he'd managed to get access to the vaults, long enough to check if there was anything that resembled the handwritten note Zara had claimed his uncle had written. Maybe it was a wild-goose chase, but despite the odds against finding a note, he couldn't forget the stark expression on Zara's face when he had tossed the shares on the bed or the raw hurt when he'd accused her. The report Walter had sent him had been just as conflicting, confirming her identity, and also confirming that— aside from the change of name—Zara was everything she claimed to be.

The first two banks had been dead ends, and he had literally turned those rooms over; this was his last chance to find the note, if it existed.

The clerk accompanied him into the vault and waited while he did a quick search of the room. The small trash can was empty. He was just about to leave when a corner of white caught his eye. A piece of paper had slipped down between the wall and the stainless steel desk used for opening safe-deposit boxes.

He fished out the piece of notepaper and went still

inside, all the hairs at his nape lifting. He would recognize Tyler's firm, slanted writing anywhere.

He read the brief note, then read it again. He tried to breathe, but his chest had closed up. Zara had been telling the truth.

And he had made a mistake, the biggest mistake of his life.

He suddenly became aware of how much time had passed. He checked his watch, thanked the clerk, then left the bank.

It took him ten minutes to reach the hotel, but he had the odd feeling that it was ten minutes too long. As he stepped into the lobby, the concierge stopped him and handed him an envelope.

Impatient to reach the suite, Damon opened the envelope as he stepped out of the elevator. He instantly recognized a copy of the letter he had instructed his lawyers to send to Zara's lawyer years before, which, if she had signed it, would have meant she relinquished any claim to the estate.

The fact that Zara had not gotten her lawyer to draft a new letter, but had obtained a copy of the old one he had originally sent to her, conveyed a message he couldn't ignore. Years ago, he had assumed Zara had refused to sign because she had wanted to keep him dangling and her options open, so she could sue for more money later on. Now he knew that her reasoning had been the exact opposite. She hadn't signed or corresponded with him because she quite simply hadn't wanted *anything* from him.

Her signature and the date seemed to jump out at him. It had been signed that afternoon, less than an hour ago, with an initialed condition that Zara would not accept the payment offered on signing or any family share certificates or payment of any kind, ever.

He unlocked the door to the suite and stepped inside and the sense of cold seemed to grow more acute, because he instantly knew that the suite was empty. He quickly searched the rooms, but Zara and Rosie were gone, and he only had himself to blame.

He had accused Zara of being deceitful and manipulative, had seen her as a pretty gold digger looking for the good life, just like her mother. Now he knew how wrong he'd been.

Raw with grief over Tyler's death, he now realized he had jumped to conclusions and bought into the media hype, but it was a fact that Tyler had been no fool when it came to judging character. He'd had zero tolerance for superficial relationships or fortune hunters, and yet he had fallen for Petra, to the point of asking her to marry him.

The fact that Petra had insisted on the prenup, then Tyler had countered by gifting Petra a 10 percent stake in the company he had loved said it all. Damon had been wrong about Petra. And at a gut level he knew he had been utterly wrong about Zara.

Too late to remember that one of the things that had attracted him to Zara had been her fierce independence, her desire to forge her own way and not lean on anyone, least of all him.

Damon found the number for the airport while he took the elevator to the underground garage. After a short conversation, during which he managed to establish that there were flights leaving for London and Dubai in the next hour, Damon terminated the call. He found his car and accelerated out into the street.

Zara's taxi was stalled in traffic.

She spoke in rapid Medinian to the driver, but he simply gesticulated. A truck had overturned on the road; they were going nowhere. Maybe in a few minutes.

Craning around, she checked the traffic lined up behind, trying to see if she could spot Damon's glossy black car. She was almost certain she had glimpsed it as she and Rosie had slipped out of the hotel, which meant he would have received the document she'd left for him and knew they had gone.

A car honked; they inched forward. Long minutes later, they idled past the overturned vegetable truck, moving at a snail's pace. She asked the driver to go faster. He gave her a blank look in the rearview mirror.

A wad of Medinian notes solved the problem. Minutes later, the taxi was zooming toward the airport at breakneck speed. The cluttered streets of Medinos finally gave way to hilly countryside dotted with goats and ancient olive groves. Lush vineyards lined with vines that were festooned with leaves and dripping with ripe black grapes signaled that the airport, situated on a plateau in the midst of the most fertile land on Medinos, was near.

Zara's phone chimed and her heart almost stopped in her chest. She checked who was calling—Damon.

She turned the phone off and held on for dear life as the taxi careened into a space outside the departures gate. After muttering her thanks and shoving more money at the driver, she scrambled out and put Rosie in the stroller. Looping her handbag over one shoulder, she grabbed her suitcase with her spare hand and headed for the desk.

She checked the overhead computer. There was a flight leaving for London in forty minutes. She pressured the attendant behind the counter to let her get on the flight, but was flatly refused. Zara checked the screen; the next flight out was an hour and twenty minutes away.

Just when she was about to give up, she saw Jorge. She called out to him, and he turned, his expression comical.

He grinned and shook his head. "So you're not too famous to talk to me today."

He held up a tabloid paper and she almost died on the spot. There was a blurry picture of her and Damon kissing in the underground garage. The janitor hadn't just overheard them, he had snapped them as well, then sold the story.

She stared at the grainy photo, her mind working quickly. She hated the notoriety of it, but for once she was going to use it. She stared at Jorge. "Now you see why I have to get off Medinos. Can you help me?"

Twenty minutes later, and after paying an exorbitant amount for tickets, she and Rosie were personally escorted to their seats. Zara had had to buy first-class seats, but for once the money hadn't mattered, and first class had fitted with her celebrity-on-the-run-from-the-paparazzi plea.

A few minutes after that, the flight taxied out, but instead of taking off, it wheeled to a halt. Apparently, there were birds on the runway. Zara's stomach hollowed out. She was beginning to wonder if they would ever get off the ground.

Twelve

Damon terminated his latest attempt to call Zara when he arrived at the airport terminal. Like every other call had, it would go straight to voice mail. He had already left a message and Zara hadn't replied, so there was no sense leaving another.

He parked and headed for departures. The flight to London was already on the tarmac waiting to depart, but the Dubai flight had yet to board. He skimmed the passengers massed in the lounge. Zara wasn't there, so she must have boarded the first flight out, which was London bound.

He called Walter. He needed confirmation of which flight Zara had taken. Walter had connections in the aviation world. If anyone could get the information, quickly, he could.

Walter called him back a few minutes later and confirmed that Zara and Rosie were on the London flight.

Jaw tight, Damon watched as the jet began moving down the runway, picking up speed. A few seconds later it was in the air. Taking out his phone again, he called Mac. He had already asked her to fuel the jet and get ready to fly, but he was aware that they would have to queue.

It took an hour to file the flight plan, another hour to get a takeoff slot. When they were finally in the air, Damon opened up the file on his laptop and read through Walter's report in detail.

Zara was Petra's daughter and, yes, there were a few wild media stories about her, but on close inspection, there wasn't a lot of substance to any of them. He studied the few photos that were included and shook his head. There was a photo of a child who was recognizably Zara, cute in plaits, and a blurred snapshot of a teenager with dark hair who could be anyone. Finally, he stared incredulously at an article entitled Angel Parties Hard. It was an article supposedly about Angel Atrides, but the photograph depicted a long-haired bottle blonde who was a complete stranger.

Grimly, Damon read on. The claims that she slept around were outright lies. He knew that for a fact because Zara had only ever slept with him. Claims that she was a fortune hunter looking for a rich husband were similarly flawed, because she had clearly never been a party girl, or dated anyone who actually had a fortune, except himself, and she'd had no compunction about ditching him.

Walter hadn't just dug for information, he had mined.

After Petra's death, Zara had been saddled with Petra's funeral expenses. Damon knew she could have taken the easy way out and accepted his money, but instead, as a student, she had paid off her mother's funeral expenses in tiny increments until the debt was cleared.

Those were not the actions of a woman who was looking for some man to bankroll her lifestyle. She hadn't *had* a lifestyle. What she'd had were debts and worry, then a child to care for—his child—and a determination to make her own way. *Without him.*

Zara had no credit cards and almost no debt, just the mortgage on her business. Somehow, in this modern day and age, she managed to make all of her purchases with cash. From what Damon could glean, despite the Swiss finishing school and the jet-setting mother, Zara only bought what she could afford, and that was mostly necessities. No designer clothing or shoes, and definitely no jewelry. That meant the diamonds were exactly what she had claimed.

Security and stability.

The final nail in the coffin was the information he already knew, but which he had stubbornly ignored. When Zara had become pregnant and could have demanded money from him, she had determinedly made her own way.

Her business was a case in point. Zara had gotten her business degree, worked and saved, gotten a loan, then opened her own business. She had accepted him as a client only because she had needed the cash flow. Then she had insisted on dealing only with Howard, making it clear that she didn't want Damon to step any further into her life.

Closing the file, Damon checked the time. They wouldn't land for several hours. He needed to sleep, but first he needed to figure out how he was going to win back Zara when he had done his level best to drive her away.

When they landed at Heathrow, it was only to find that Zara and Rosie had caught a last-minute connection to Los Angeles.

Mac yawned. "What do we do now?"

Damon noted Zara's arrival time in LA. He didn't know if she would take a connecting flight from there, or choose to stop over. What mattered was that she appeared to be heading home.

"We get some dinner, get some sleep and then go home."

Zara paid the taxi driver, who obligingly wheeled her luggage through her front gate while Zara carried Rosie.

Rosie was not happy. She had been fractious on the red-eye flight from LA to Auckland, which had taken thirteen long, horrible hours. Her lashes were spiky from crying and her cheeks were red. Zara suspected that she was cutting another tooth, which was, literally, the last straw.

Blinking against the brilliance of the morning sun, when her body clock wanted it to be night, she unlocked the front door and carried Rosie through to her room and settled her in her crib.

Feeling dizzy with exhaustion, she trudged back out to the porch to claim her luggage, only to be buttonholed by Edna Cross, who was waiting on the step with a woman's magazine. "It says in here that you're the daughter of that famous supermodel—"

"Petra Hunt. She was my mother."

Edna blinked. "That explains why that blonde reporter was hanging around. I called the police on her."

The sun seemed to shine a little brighter. "Vanessa Gardiner. Way to go, Mrs. Cross."

"If she comes back, I can slap a harassment charge on her if you like."

"Will that work?"

"Probably not, but it'll make her life difficult."

Zara's chest suddenly felt a little tight. "Thank you, Mrs. Cross."

"You can call me Edna. Just being neighborly. If there's anything else you need, let me know."

Zara watched as Edna ambled back to her house. Across the road another neighbor—old Mr. Harris, who was out washing his car—paused and lifted a hand. It was a strange moment to feel that, finally, she belonged somewhere.

After depositing her bags in the sitting room and opening up a few windows to air out the house, she called Molly to see how she was coping. Apparently, owing to the media attention, they'd had an influx of new clients and there was a long list of new job applicants to screen. The magazine article, and a number of tabloid follow-ups, all of which Molly assured her she had hated, had done wonders for business. She'd had to take on one of their temps to cope with the increased workload and Harriet was proving to be a real gem.

Molly paused. "Are you really Angel Atrides and a *contessa*?"

Zara smothered a yawn. Now that she was home, tiredness was closing in. All she wanted to do was sleep. "Yes and yes. But the *contessa* thing is a bit like the sheikh taxi driver who just dropped me off. Without an estate and a huge bank account, it doesn't actually mean anything."

"Hmm. Harriet thinks it's an asset. She's had a lot of experience with public relations and thinks it could provide an important point of difference for the agency. Not to mention an opportunity to harness the media attention in a good way."

After a brief discussion, Zara decided that with Harriet in the mix, she could take a few days off and disappear from sight until the media furor died down. Molly instantly offered Zara the use of a family beach house on Auckland's west coast.

Even though she was exhausted, Zara decided to leave straightaway. They were already packed and even though Rosie was still out of sorts, at least if they went for a drive in the car, she might fall asleep.

Two hours later, with Rosie bathed, changed and fed, all of her luggage transferred to the car and enough groceries to last a few days, Zara drove until she found the small cottage, which was situated on a windswept cliff overlooking a wild stretch of coastline. She found the key, which was sitting beneath a flowerpot, unlocked the door and began ferrying bags inside.

Rosie, thankfully, had fallen into a deep slumber, so Zara gently transferred her from her car seat to a portable crib she had managed to borrow from a friend.

The sun was sliding into the sea by the time she made herself a sandwich and a cup of tea for dinner and collapsed into a faded armchair. She woke hours later to find that she had fallen dead asleep in the chair and was now freezing cold. She blinked at the noise that had woken her and realized it was her phone.

Retrieving the cell from the kitchen table, she checked the screen. Her heart slammed hard against her chest. Damon had tried to call her for about the twentieth time.

She stared at her voice mail, which also registered a message from Damon. What she really needed to do was throw the whole phone, which belonged to Magnum Security, away.

Switching on a light, she checked on Rosie who was warmly cuddled up beneath thick blankets and searched out a sweater and a warm pair of socks for herself. She checked her watch as she filled a kettle with water so she could make a hot drink and was shocked to see it was only ten o'clock. She was about to turn the kettle on when she thought she heard a noise. Frowning, she listened hard. There was a road not far from the cottage, which led to a popular beach suburb, so there was traffic, but this didn't sound like a car.

Another sound, this one more distinct, made her stiffen. Suddenly wondering if a reporter had tracked her here and was even now sneaking up to the window to snap a photo of her, she grabbed the kettle, which was full of cold water. Instead of walking out the front door and being an instant target for anyone with a camera, she padded out the back door and walked quietly around the small cottage.

A low sound behind her spun her around. Damon's gaze locked with hers, but it was too late to stop the flight of the kettle which, out of sheer fright, she'd flung in the direction of the sound.

He caught the kettle, but water sprayed, drenching his dark jersey and jeans. "Remind me to put you on one of my security teams." He wiped water from his face. "No, cancel that. Walter said you should be running a war. I'm in complete agreement. You can run the teams."

Zara rubbed her arms against the biting cold and tried to ignore the fact that even dripping wet and probably just as tired as she, Damon looked certifiably gorgeous. "What are you doing here?"

"Looking for you."

"Why?"

"I found the note from Tyler. It was in the bank, like you said."

Her heart pounded at that, but she refused to let herself hope. "So you believed *Tyler*."

Turning on her heel, she walked back into the house, but despite every effort to be indifferent to Damon her pulse was hammering and she was hopelessly aware of him. A little desperately she wondered what it took to get rid of the zing of attraction, or the crazy, heady feeling of hope springing to life again.

If she let herself hope, she thought ruthlessly, she would only set herself up to be hurt again and she was over being hurt.

She flicked on lights, illuminating the tiny rooms with their jumble of mismatched furniture, the miniature kitchen that fitted two or three people at the most. When Damon stepped into the kitchen, the room seemed to shrink even more.

He put the kettle on the bench. "I'm sorry I frightened you. I thought I heard someone around the back."

"That would be me!"

"As it turned out."

Okay, so he had been protecting her. She tried not to feel happy about that as she filled the kettle with water again and put it on to boil. Feeling crazily nervous to have Damon so close, in her personal space when she never thought he would be again, she busied herself finding a towel.

In the meantime, Damon had peeled out of his jersey, which was soaked, and hung it over the back of a chair. Zara tried not to notice his bronzed biceps, or the way the T-shirt clung across his chest. She concentrated, instead, on making tea. After he had blotted the worst of the moisture from his T-shirt, Damon tossed the damp towel over the back of another chair.

She poured tea and handed him a mug. His gaze caught hers. "You were right. I didn't believe you, and for the reason you said. I have difficulty with…trust."

Leaning against the bench, he began to talk about his childhood, the words at first hard and slow, then flowing more smoothly. Ben had given Zara a brief outline of how Damon's life had gone, but he had barely scratched the surface. By the time Damon had finished, the tea had gone cold.

Zara set her mug down. "But growing up, you must have realized your parents' marriage was…dysfunctional."

He set his mug down, the drink untasted. "Maybe, but I wasn't exactly brought up under normal circumstances even after they died. Tyler was the closest thing Ben and I had to a real father—"

"And he was a confirmed bachelor until he met my mother."

"Then there was my stint in the army. I'm not making excuses. I'm just trying to explain why I've been so resistant to a real relationship."

Her head came up. For a long, vibrating moment she thought she'd heard wrong. "What do you mean by a real relationship?"

He caught the fingers of one hand and drew her close. "I mean you and me and a second chance."

"Why? Because of Rosie?"

He pulled her closer still. "You know it's not about Rosie. I love her, she's my daughter and finding her jolted me. But it was falling for you and losing you that made me realize how empty my life was. I've been trying to control my relationships but that approach never worked. Lily hit it right on the button. If I refused to risk myself and go out on a limb for someone else, I couldn't expect to be in a relationship."

"Which explains why you walked away from me when you found me in Dunedin over a year ago!"

His gaze locked with hers. "I didn't say I wasn't stubborn. But, when you came back to town, it didn't take me long to track you down. And once I did, I tried to stay close. Why do you think I kept employing your temps?"

She tried not to drown in the molten heat of his gaze. "I did wonder." She suddenly remembered the question that had gnawed at her earlier. "By the way, how *did* you find me this time?"

"GPS. You've got a company phone."

She tried to breathe, but it seemed to be getting awfully hot and close in the tiny kitchen. "I was thinking of throwing the SIM card away."

He grinned. "Why do you think I got here so fast?"

He reached into his pocket and she caught the glint of something shiny. Her heart slammed hard in her chest. At first she thought he was returning the earrings to her, but she was wrong. It was an engagement ring.

Suddenly all the vulnerabilities that had gone with loving Damon surged back. If they were going to do this, she couldn't bear it if it all fell apart again.

Damon went down on one knee, with difficulty, because the space between the kitchen counter and the small table was so cramped. One shoulder bumped against a shelf of pots, sending a lid spinning onto the tiled floor. When Zara stepped back to allow him more room, a chair crashed to the floor. The noise woke Rosie, who began to make cute sounds in her room. It was bedlam and it was the most romantic thing that had ever happened.

Damon gripped her hand. "I don't want to lose you again. I've loved you from the first moment you stepped into that interview room. The problem was, you made me feel too much and I had gotten used to closing down and looking for reasons not to trust. I'm sorry, babe—I didn't mean to hurt you. I just didn't have the courage to admit that I needed you. When you walked out on me this time, I knew that I loved you. It was too late, but I finally understood exactly what I wanted. You, Rosie and the home we can make together, if only you'll trust *me*."

Damon grasped her left hand. "Will you marry me, for better or worse, for richer or poorer?"

The vows of the marriage service made Zara's throat close up so that when she spoke her voice was husky. "That's all I ever wanted. I just hadn't thought it was possible."

But as Damon slid the engagement ring onto the third finger of her left hand, and rose up to kiss her—knocking his mug of tea into the sink—she suddenly realized that it was more than possible.

Two people truly, honestly in love, and their baby.

It was real and just a little chaotic, and she knew it was going to be *perfect*.

* * * * *

#2617 MOST ELIGIBLE TEXAN
Texas Cattleman's Club: Bachelor Auction
by Jules Bennett
Tycoon Matt Galloway's going up on the bachelor auction block, but there's only one woman he wants bidding on him—his best friend's widow. Then his plans to seduce the gorgeous single mom get *really* complicated when old secrets come to light...

#2618 THE BILLIONAIRE'S LEGACY
Billionaires and Babies • by Reese Ryan
When tech billionaire Benjamin Bennett returns home for his cousin's wedding, a passionate weekend with his former crush—his older sister's best friend, Sloane Sutton—results in *two* surprises. But can he get past Sloane's reasons for refusing to marry him for the twins' sakes?

#2619 TEMPT ME IN VEGAS
by Maureen Child
Cooper Hayes should have inherited his partner's half of their Vegas hotel empire. Instead, the man's secret daughter is now part owner! The wide-eyed beauty is ill suited for wheeling and dealing, and Cooper *will* buy her out. But not before he takes her to his bed...

#2620 HOT CHRISTMAS KISSES
Love in Boston • by Joss Wood
International power broker Matt Edwards can never be more than an on-again, off-again hookup to DJ Winston. But when he moves to Boston and becomes part of her real life—carrying secrets with him—their red-hot chemistry explodes. Will they finally face the feelings they've long denied?

#2621 RANCHER UNTAMED
Cole's Hill Bachelors • by Katherine Garbera
When wealthy rancher Diego Velasquez donates one night to the highest bidder, he's bought by a nanny! But after one fiery encounter, beautiful Pippa slips away, driven by secrets she can't reveal. Now this Texan vows he'll learn the truth and have her back in his arms!

#2622 THE BOYFRIEND ARRANGEMENT
Millionaires of Manhattan • by Andrea Laurence
Sebastian said yes to Harper's fake-boyfriend scheme—because he couldn't resist! Now, as her date at a destination wedding, every dance, every touch, every kiss makes him want more. But when a blackmailer reveals everything, will they choose to turn this false romance into something real?

When tech billionaire Benjamin Bennett returns home
for his cousin's wedding, a passionate weekend with his
former crush—his elder sister's best friend
Sloane Sutton—results in two surprises. But can he get
past Sloane's reasons for refusing to marry him
for the twins' sakes?

Read on for a sneak peek of
The Billionaire's Legacy by Reese Ryan,
part of the Billionaires and Babies series!

Benjamin Bennett was a catch by anyone's standards—
even before you factored in his healthy bank account.
But he was her best friend's little brother. And though he
was all grown-up now, he was just a kid compared to her.

Flirting with Benji would start tongues wagging all
over Magnolia Lake. Not that she cared what they thought
of her. But if the whole town started talking, it would
make things uncomfortable for the people she loved.

"Thanks for the dance."

Benji lowered their joined hands but didn't let go.
Instead, he leaned down, his lips brushing her ear and his
well-trimmed beard gently scraping her neck. "Let's get
out of here."

It was a bad idea. A really bad idea.

Her cheeks burned. "But it's your cousin's wedding."

He nodded toward Blake, who was dancing with his

bride, Savannah, as their infant son slept on his shoulder. The man was in complete bliss.

"I doubt he'll notice I'm gone. Besides, you'd be rescuing me. If Jeb Dawson tells me one more time about his latest invention—"

"Okay, okay." Sloane held back a giggle as she glanced around the room. "You need to escape as badly as I do. But there's no way we're leaving here together. It'd be on the front page of the newspaper by morning."

"Valid point." Benji chuckled. "So meet me at the cabin."

"The cabin on the lake?" She had so many great memories of weekends spent there.

It would just be two old friends catching up on each other's lives. Nothing wrong with that.

She repeated it three times in her head. But there was nothing friendly about the sensations that danced along her spine when he'd held her in his arms and pinned her with that piercing gaze.

"Okay. Maybe we can catch up over a cup of coffee or something."

"Or something." The corner of his sensuous mouth curved in a smirk.

A shiver ran through her as she wondered, for the briefest moment, how his lips would taste.

Don't miss
The Billionaire's Legacy *by Reese Ryan,*
part of the Billionaires and Babies series!

Available October 2018 wherever
Harlequin® Desire books and ebooks are sold.

www.Harlequin.com